Truth Heals the Heart

By:
Kathy Roberts

Copyright 2014 Kathy Roberts
Cover Artist: Desiree DeOrto

For Breanna,
Never forget you always have
more to offer!

TABLE OF CONTENTS

Preface

I so enjoyed writing about Princess Katrina and Prince Nicholas Andrew Markus Jamison V, that when I finished their story's beginning, I got even more excited to tell more about them. Scars of the Heart took them from tragedy and near loss of life, to a world of romance, love and a devotion that would last. They battled evil and triumphed. They survived all obstacles thrown at them, because they did it together for each other because of a love born from deep within instead of a fleeting passion that overtakes so many people who "think" they're in love. Real Love Lasts!

Markus and Katrina have more adventure in this book, their love continues to grow and their passion increases as it should between a husband and wife. Many changes are coming their way, but with every trial, they work together to triumph again. The first book told of the scars in their hearts, literal, emotional and spiritual. This book continues their story and shows how, no matter how deep, those scars can heal and love can prevail.

With all that said, it is a stand-alone book as well.
I hope you enjoy them as much as I have.

Again, first and foremost, Thanks to God
always for everything in my life!

To the people in my life who've been an
inspiration to me. I know you are and were a
great part of who I am. Precious saints of God
who demonstrated how through our faith in
God, His love in our hearts and pursuing the
will of God and trusting His plan, all our scars
can heal.

Just to name a few:

Earl & Agnes Carnes, my grandparents (deceased)
James & Ora Wyant, my "other" grandparents(deceased)
Elder Ray & Pansy Sovine, my parents
Junior (deceased)& Linda Sowards, my "other" parents
Aunt Mary Sowards (deceased)
Aunt Lila Sowards (deceased)
Betty Setliff
Elder Tony Cooper (deceased)
Elder Paul Harbour (deceased)
Hugh & Nanny Meadows (deceased)
Bill (deceased) & Sophie Woodard
Elder Kermit & Margie Cunningham (deceased)
Elder Bill Blackshire
Elder Carl & Nelma Cooper (deceased)
John & Winnie Davis (deceased)
Hazel Davis (deceased)
Elma Davis (deceased)
Jack (deceased) & Bertha Sowards
Romie (deceased)& Julia McCallister

Chapter 1 - Ecstasy

It was a glorious morning. Last night had not been like any other night Katrina had spent with Markus. She was his wife now and she could and did give all of herself to him. With her mother gone, she really didn't have anyone to give her instructions in this area. She was as innocent as a sixteen year old girl could be and Markus knew this so he went as slowly as he could and was as gentle as he could be because he wanted to cause her as little pain as possible. It wasn't very long before she was as enraptured as he. His patience and guidance was paying off. She responded to his slightest touch and he reached the same heights of ecstasy as she did before the climax and release of themselves to the intensity of their lovemaking. Markus was so happy Katrina had made him wait until they were married. It made their new life all the more pleasurable. They were on this ride together. He had never reached this height with any other woman. Love really does make the difference. He certainly loved her with all his heart and she loved him just as much.

Katrina scooted away from Markus just enough to look at his face. He had never looked so satisfied or complete since she'd met him. If the rest of her life is going to be like last night, she'd die with a smile on her face. No wonder so many are tempted beyond their resolve. She didn't know how it happened, but he was more handsome this morning than he was at the wedding. She was so caught up in admiring his features and contemplating last night that she didn't even notice he had awakened and was watching her. She jumped a little when he spoke "My love, you are more beautiful than ever before. I can't believe the places you took me to last night. Let's get married every day so every night can be like that." She laughed "I know what you mean sweetheart, but I don't think we have to remarry every day to have nights like last night. I'm ready, able, and more than willing to repeat last night's performance every night of our lives. I love you so much more than I did yesterday and I didn't think that was possible. I know my love will continue to grow more and more with every passing day. Markus, you have made me the happiest woman in the world." Now it was his turn to chuckle. "Well, I've made you a woman, that's for sure. I am starving after all that love making, let's get some robes on and have some breakfast."

At that instant, there was a knock on the door. "Yes" Markus answered. It was Anne. "Your Highness, your mother has instructed I bring you both breakfast in bed. May I come in?" she asked "Of course." He answered as soon as he made sure Katrina was covered. Anne carried in a huge tray of food and set it on the table by his side of the bed. "Your mother instructed you two should stay in bed all day and be undisturbed except for meals as this was your day. Should you need anything, just ring. Otherwise, I'll be back with lunch. I think she's anxious for some grandbabies." She glanced at Katrina as she said this and of course Katrina blushed. "If you have any needs My Lady, just ring." She smiled at Katrina knowingly and left the room.

"Perfect timing!" Markus exclaimed. "Look what a spread." He started filling a plate for her as he took a couple bites of fruit from the tray. He handed her plate over and she immediately began gobbling her food down. "I can't believe how hungry I am." she said with a mouthful of food. "I'm sorry sweetheart, but I can't stop eating. Oh my, it's heavenly and so delicious." He poured her some tea and handed it over before she choked on her food. They slowed down, but didn't stop until every bite was gone. "Markus, I'm going to be the fattest bride in history." She said as she rubbed her stomach. Markus pulled her closer and rubbed her stomach himself. "I don't care how fat you are, or how big your stomach gets with babies inside. I'll always love you and will always think you are the most beautiful woman alive." "Oh Markus, you are the sweetest man I've ever met." She replied. "Now, let's go to sleep" he told her "and we'll examine your body again later." Katrina giggled and snuggled close.

Katrina did not immediately go to sleep. She lay there thinking about her life. She had gone from being an orphan to a princess in a matter of two years. When her father was murdered, she thought her life was over. She had no family left, save an uncle. Her father had been her life since her mother and brother had died of the fever. She'd also thought herself a murderer for those two years. Killing in self-defense and vengeance, the man who murdered her father, she thought. Life had a strange way of chewing a person's life all up, and then spitting them out and making things turn out ok in the end. The connection made that night had brought her and Markus so close and ultimately madly in love with each other and married. They had survived each other and much more adversity in that short amount of time than most people face in a lifetime.

One thing she was sure of, she would never be alone again. Markus was her champion, her protector, her husband, her supporter, her comfort, her friend, and her lover.

She reached her hand across his chest and placed her fingers on the scar that had become such a comfort to her and fell asleep.

They repeated this routine at lunch and dinner Each time they were more exhausted and more in love. Each time more famished and consuming everything on the tray provided.

Each time holding each other close before falling asleep again, only to wake in a few hours to begin again. Katrina was sure she would not be able to walk the next morning; not that she'd want to, she'd love to stay in this bed for the rest of their lives and just live in their own small world. But alas, he was the prince and heir to the throne, so that was not to be. They both had duties to perform and things to attend to, but they had today...all alone and all to themselves.

Katrina knew that while every night might not be as magical as last night, she knew they would always share an intimacy born of love before passion. And they had both proven they'd do whatever was necessary to protect each other, the queen, and their kingdom. They not only would be good for each other, they would be great rulers over their country. Katrina was pretty sure they'd be great parents too.

Chapter 2 – A Trip to Prison

"Good morning, my love." Markus greeted Katrina when he woke her up with a kiss. "I've rang for Anne and she's preparing your bath as we speak. I've had mine and will be going to breakfast in a couple minutes. I have to make arrangements for us to get things moving back to Castle Jamison.

I also have to check on Alexander and make sure he's absolutely secure before we can go home. I have to interview the guards and make sure none show any signs of allegiance to him. We have to make sure he's fed, but we don't' have to allow him company or even allow the guards to talk to him." Markus explained. "I feel sorry for him." Katrina spoke softly. "He really is so much like you. He's charming and of course handsome, but he really does have a heart and love for this country. If only his heart were not made so bitter. If only he didn't feel he had a claim to the throne. When he was pretending to be you, I really liked him and sometimes found myself forgetting I wasn't with you. He was so attentive and well just loveable. I really wish there were something we could do to turn him around. Prison is such an awful place for an active man like him to be kept caged." She continued. "I can't imagine being in prison." Markus replied. "But until we can think of something, it is what he'll have to suffer for his actions. I can't trust him with your safety."

"Lady Patrice has been sent home in shame to her father and will never be allowed at court again. She's lost her title and cannot marry anyone of title. It's sad, really, I believe she was swayed and being so young didn't know how to handle the pressure she was put under. I think she may have loved her cousin as well and wanted to gain his favor. I hate it most because she was so good with mother, but she can't be trusted. We could all have been killed." "Well, he is the second most handsome man in the kingdom." Katrina began with a smile. "A young girl's head could easily be turned by a man so persuasive.

What about the informant at Castle Jamison?" she asked. "Have they been found?" "I sent Henry back as soon as the wedding was over and I just received word this morning that he did find the culprit, or culprits, I should say. A kitchen maid who succumbed to his wiles, her brother who is one of our livery staff and one of the butlers were involved in giving him information. They all said they thought it was a game I was playing with everyone. Since I was in the middle of such a charade with kidnapping you and all; they just thought this was part of all that. Keeping "me" informed of everyone's comings and goings so I could make sure no one revealed my secret to you." Henry believes them; and I trust Henry, he's a good judge of character. They've all been disciplined and know that any infraction will lead to dismissal or even trial for treason. I think we're good keeping them all on."

"Oh Markus, it's been such an ordeal with so many people being hurt. I am amazed we've all escaped with only minor bruises and have been able to find and eliminate our enemies. It's just such a shame and waste. I wish our lives were not tainted with this horrible past, but I suppose that's what makes us who we are." She said.

"As bad as it is for some, especially Alexander, his cohorts and Lady Patrice, it could have been much worse. They all could have hanged. I think we've been more than fair with them all." Markus explained.

"Now to your bath woman. I promise to have one with you tomorrow morning. I hope to be back for lunch. I wish to spend some time with mother before going home, and I think we have a dinner tonight and luncheon tomorrow before we can leave." When he finished speaking, he kissed her again, rather longingly and left her sitting on the side of the bed wanting more. How in the world could she want more after the day and two nights of lovemaking they'd just experienced? Ah, she loved that man with all her heart, mind, and body.

Alexander had not had so pleasant a couple days. He had a foolproof plan, how could it have gone wrong? The woman! That's what changed his plans. The exquisite Katrina had turned his head with her beauty, charm, and innocence. With the body of a goddess and that long flowing auburn hair, she was truly stunning. Now Markus had her and he was stuck in prison. He'd come so close to achieving his vengeance and a beautiful prize to boot, but now he had nothing again and wasn't just banished this time, but locked away. He didn't even have a window in his cell. There was one across from his door, but his door only had a small slit and he could just see the sky and the mountains beyond in the distance. His cohorts were the only ones nearby and they were barely within earshot. If they tried to call out to talk, the guards would make them shut up. He was going to spend a miserable life if he didn't figure some way to get out of there. He'd only been there two days, but he'd searched every corner of his cell, every inch of the floor for a weakness, any weakness that could be manipulated into a way out. The guards didn't even have to open the door for his meals. There was a space at the bottom of the door to slide his tray through. He would go mad if this is how he'd have to spend every day of his life. Nothing to do, nothing to read, no one to talk to. How could this have happened to him? He was only trying to get what was his. He'd been cheated out of the throne and it just wasn't fair! He liked Markus, but he didn't want him to have his throne, no more than Markus would want him to have Katrina!

Just then, Markus appeared at the slit in the door. He'd heard the noise and when he looked up, he knew those eyes. He saw them every day when he looked into the mirror. They were identical. Even the queen could not tell them apart. No wonder people thought they had the same father since they had different mothers.

"What do you want? Come to gloat?" Alexander snarled at him. "No I came to talk to you" Markus began. "I know you feel the kingdom should be yours, but there are circumstances you are not aware of. I'm hoping to make you understand so you will not be so bitter. We were such good friends once. We could finish each other's thoughts. We played like brothers and even as teenagers we fought for the same girls, we were inseparable. I miss you Alexander. Don't you miss me any at all? Has hatred consumed you?" Markus asked.

"I do miss you. You are my brother, not in name, but in heart. I do often think of those times, but I cannot deny my right, left me by my father. I have to try to win back what is mine. I never really wanted to hurt your mother, she was so much of a mother to me as I never knew mine, but I was coached and guided from early on by my father. It seemed he was obsessed with teaching me what I needed to know to become a good king. I remember when I was little, he'd say your mother gave her life to give you life and we are going to make the most of it. Sometimes he would cry. I know he missed her so much. He would explain in detail and make me memorize laws and rules. Names of the lawyers, the people at court, every title and landholder, all the proper etiquette, everything a king would need to know. I had to learn to ride, joust, sword-fight and to shoot a bow. I've been fully trained in war as well as the pleasantries of court. He made me solve problems, so I could give advice and rule wisely. I've had more grooming and training than you have Markus. My father was next in line for the throne. It is rightfully mine."

When Alexander finished he hung his head and Markus began. "I know you feel that way, but you attacked my mother before you found out the entire story. You were banished and would not listen to anyone or anything; well today you are going to listen. I know your father was hard on you and taught you well, but he was hard on himself. He blamed himself for your mother's death. Had she not gotten with child, she wouldn't have died. They loved each other so much; a child was all they both wanted. Someone to carry on the kingdom. Mother says they spent many hours together as they were both expecting children at the same time. Your mother would tell her how she could imagine the crown on her baby's head. Not even knowing if she carried a boy or not. She just knew it. She would tell your father every day that he had to spend all the time he could with you because she wanted her baby to be a better king than his father, and his father was going to be one of the best ever. She had some difficulty early on and they were afraid something would happen to the baby. She would spend hours praying for her child. She loved your father with all her heart, but she wanted this baby for him more than anything. You need to know of their love and compassion, their longing for the best for you, and you need to know how your father really died." As Markus finished those words, Alexander looked up again. "I thought he died in battle? That's what I was told. Is there more?" He asked.

"The reason my mother took the throne and made me heir was because your father could not take any more loneliness. He had gone to battle along with my father and our grandfather, the king. When the battle was in its worst part and had lasted far longer than they all expected; the stench of death was strong in the air and dying men were longing for home and their families. Your father caught that fever and wanted more than anything to be with his beloved wife. He didn't care about living any more. All he knew was killing and death. They say many men deserted that day. They ran, heading for home. None of them were named traitors; they were all named heroes because of the horrific nature of it all. It's a wonder any of them kept their sanity, but those with great loss already, just could not handle it any more. Because he ran, he lost his claim to the throne and that eliminated his line as well. He wasn't a traitor, he was sick in the mind, but law is law. The king could protect his name, but something had to be done to end his line for the throne. He was mortally wounded, but they brought him back to the palace to make the decree for his successor. My mother was the one blamed for coercing him into giving it to her and her son because they did not want to ruin your father's good name. So upon the king's death, that made mother queen and me heir. There were too many men present when those ran, for the throne to pass to you; but grandfather decreed the illness was the cause and all the men declared heroes.

Alexander, mother did not steal the throne, it was rightfully hers, she just bore the burden of people thinking she took it and maybe even had her brother put to death. I'll send the captain to talk to you, if you'd like. He will tell you the same story if I give him permission. None of them were to dispute the king's decree,

so they all kept silent even knowing the queen was being accused of acts she didn't commit."
"STOP IT! STOP YOUR LIES!" Alexander interrupted. "You will make up any story to protect yourselves and try to make me believe I'm not heir to the throne! I'll have none of it. You will NOT dishonor my father! You will NOT convince me of your lies! Your mother stole my kingdom and until I die, I will keep trying to get it back!" When he'd finished screaming at Markus, he turned his back to the door and screamed once more "GO! LEAVE ME ALONE AND DO NOT COME BACK!"

Markus did not speak another word, but turned quietly and left. Maybe he'd send the captain to visit Alexander in a month or so. After he had time to calm down and really ponder on what Markus had told him. He would love for Alexander to believe him and really turn his life around. He would love to spend time with him like before. He hated keeping him in prison, but for now, there was no other choice. It was with a heavy heart that he told the guards again, no one but the captain could visit him and no one was to talk to him. He was to have food and clothing, but nothing more.

Chapter 3 – Moving On

When he returned to the palace, it was just before lunch time, so he hurried to his mother's sitting room where he knew she and Katrina would be waiting for him. She had filled Katrina in on the story while Markus was talking to Alexander. "Well, she asked?" Markus sat down rather slowly. "He would have no part of it. He thinks we're making up lies, trying to destroy his father's name to get him to give up his attempts to gain the throne. I tried mother, I really did. I love Alexander and I miss him. We were so close growing up, like brothers. I wish that had never changed." She watched him as he spoke. He too had lost much in his life. He lost his father and his best friend, who was like his brother, all at the same time. She could only hope for his future. He had a beautiful new wife and hopefully would have many children. Unlike his mother, who had only Markus. "Come dear" she spoke softly, "let's not dwell on the past too much. Alexander will have a lot of time to think in prison and you have a new bride here waiting to share her life with you. She will fill your house with laughter and joy, with many children and love will abound. Cheer up Markus, time heals all wounds and everyone has scars of the heart, some are just deeper than others, and some are harder to heal." They headed down to lunch and the conversation lightened up considerably. They were discussing the future. Markus had sent orders to spruce up the nursery as he had high hopes of delivering an heir within the year. They all laughed. Katrina was excited at the prospect, but the queen was hoping more than any that she would have grandchildren soon. It would spur the whole kingdom. Everyone gets excited when a baby is born, but when a royal is born, it's a country wide event.

As they sat down, the queen began "Now on to business, this will probably be our last moments alone before you leave for Castle Jamison. We have a luncheon tomorrow with all the lords. They need to see the strong union you two have. They need to know our country is moving forward, that everyone is as safe as possible and there is a strong solid heir to the throne with plans to produce a long line of heirs for many years. They need to know our expectations of them as far as taxes and tribute. We will be selecting a new lady in waiting for me and Katrina will need to select two young ladies in waiting for herself."

"I'll need someone with some experience to show me the proper things to do at court." Katrina began. "Darling, you have nothing to prove, you were exquisite at court and the street fair. You are loved by all and you know how to be a princess. You also know how to communicate and mix with the commoners.

You are a rare find in a woman. I think you'll have no trouble teaching the young ladies how to act at court and imparting some much needed wisdom to them as well. I know you're very young, Katrina, but you are wise beyond your years." The queen smiled as she spoke those words and Katrina knew she was very sincere about it. Not just because Katrina was instrumental in saving Markus, the queen's life, and the throne, but because she saw the qualities in her that she wanted in a wife for her son and in the future queen of her country.

It was a beautiful luncheon and so nice to be more private for a change. They had been through so much, they just needed to be together, safe and sound and to know each was there for the other, all the time. Katrina knew in her heart she was the queen's daughter, not just her son's wife. She knew she had earned as much respect as the general of her army and she knew that she loved her and would feel indebted to her for the rest of her life. She didn't need to be, Katrina felt as if she'd only done what had to be done and didn't deserve any gratitude for doing the right thing. Still it was good to have family again. Her uncle had been wonderful and would always have a special place in her heart for taking her in when she'd been orphaned. He was just like a father to her and she loved him dearly; but finally a mother and now a husband and soon, she hoped, there would be children in her life.

Markus asked if Katrina would like to take a ride after lunch and she jumped at the chance. Some good fresh air and an exhilarating ride would be wonderful. So when lunch was over, Markus kissed his mother's cheek and told her they'd be off. They quickly changed and headed for the stables. It was a beautiful day and they thoroughly enjoyed their ride. Markus pointed out more estates and gave her information on the lords and ladies who resided there. She seemed to just absorb any information he gave her. She truly wanted to learn about the kingdom and everyone in it and she was doing just that. "Markus, it's so hard to believe one day we'll rule the kingdom." She said pensively. "My life has changed so drastically in just the short time I've lived, I can only imagine what's in store for our future." "As long as you are with me, I don't care what else the future holds. Together we can handle anything that comes our way. I think we've proven that already. Our country has been at peace for several years now, since the war where Alexander's father was killed and mother became queen. She's been a very good queen Katrina, but I know you'll be a better one. I'm sorry I missed the street fair. That was a good idea Alexander had and I'm glad you enjoyed it and want to keep it going. It will be a nice way to celebrate and announce events in our lives, like babies." He grinned. Katrina leaned over for a kiss and he just scooped her up and over to his horse for a good long one. "Let's head back and see if we can work on those babies some more." He murmured through a kiss. She smiled and very sweetly answered, "Yes, my lord, whatever you wish." He laughed aloud, reached for the reins of her horse and then headed out at a trot, back to the palace, with Katrina still firmly planted in his lap.

When they arrived back at the palace, there was no time for play. Katrina had to get ready rather quickly for the ladies presentation at court. With the help of the queen, Katrina would choose her ladies in waiting. The queen would know their skills and recommend about six for Katrina to choose from. Then it would be up to Katrina to see who's personality matched her best.

It was a fun evening for everyone. Once they were chosen all were invited to dinner with their families. Had circumstances been different in her life, Katrina may well have been on the list of ladies in waiting as her family was titled as well. There was one particular girl from her home town that caught Katrina's eye. She got the go ahead from the queen and chose her as her first. Lady Penelope of Manchester and she chose Lady Alicia of Scotsburn as her second. After the ladies had been chosen and just before dinner they had a surprise guest come in. Nanny Gertrude. She was over ninety and had delivered every baby born in the palace since Markus' great grandfather. She was the most trusted nurse in the kingdom. She'd delivered Markus and Alexander on the same day. Everyone knew her or of her and her name was always spoken of with reverence. She asked to meet Katrina and explained that since the day Markus was born, she hadn't done all the work in delivering as her age was catching up with her, but she had been in attendance and supervised all births since then. She also explained that if she lived long enough, she'd be supervising Katrina's children's births as well. It was the greatest honor that could be bestowed upon her to deliver the royalty of the kingdom. She was charming to talk to and Katrina liked her very much and told her she'd be delighted to have such experience in the room taking care of her and her babies as they were born.

There really was a lot of details in running a country and some of it was fun like tonight and some was tedious, but it all went hand in hand so she'd suffer the more torturous to be able to enjoy the treats it afforded as well.

After dinner, Markus and Katrina lay awake and talked about the day's events, Nanny Gertrude and all the babies they were going to have. Markus was sure the first would be a daughter, who looked just like her mother. She'd be the second most beautiful female in the country. Then Katrina would have to step up her game and deliver him three or four male heirs before she could have another girl. Katrina laughed and told him she didn't wield that much power. Her only power was over him and he would just have to make sure he deposited boys or girls in whatever order he wanted them. He told her he was glad she'd chosen a lady from Manchester, it would give her semblance of home and it would be more fun for them to do her shopping there. He also told her she'd better get that dressmaker working on some clothes she could wear while carrying the babies, and a whole assortment of baby clothes too. Katrina promised to take a trip there next week and get things started, just in case.

They'd better get some rest because after tomorrow's events, they'd be heading home to Castle Jamison bright and early the next morning. Katrina had pleasant dreams of that place as she drifted off to sleep. There'd been no danger from outside the castle walls, only from the man she'd married with all his charades trying to get her to love a man who'd kidnapped her without knowing he was her betrothed. She understood, but what a long game he played. She'd have fallen head over heels in love with him without all that. He just needed to know it was real, just like she had needed to know when saying I do.

Chapter 4 – Castle Jamison

It was good to be home. Anne had the staff clean the castle from top to bottom in their absence, especially the nursery. She had them at the ready as Markus and Katrina pulled up in her beautiful white coach, to unload their luggage and show the ladies their quarters and where everything was kept so they could perform their duties. She announced dinner could be served as quickly as they'd like. She knew they'd be tired and hungry from their trip. Markus took one look at Katrina and told Anne they'd take dinner in 15 minutes, then would be bathing and retiring for the evening.

At the doorway, he scooped her up into his arms and carried her over the thresh hold. "My bride is home." He said smiling and all the staff applauded. He lightly set her down inside the door and kissed her gingerly while they all watched. He wanted them all to know how much he loved his wife and how much she loved him. He was sure there was no question from those who'd witnessed his protection of her during the time she didn't know he was her espoused, and after when she'd declared her love for him; but he didn't want any doubts.

As they ascended the stairs to their room to freshen up, Katrina asked if she looked that bad. "Quite the contrary, my love, you look wonderful. That's why we're hurrying to have dinner, then I'm taking you to bed for the rest of the evening." Markus explained with a grin and a light smack on her rump. She giggled and hurried on into their room.

She'd barely entered when Lady Penelope knocked at her door and asked if she could help her get ready for dinner. "Not this time, Lord Markus will be assisting me. He's quite good at it and truly likes to do so when time permits. Go ahead and get settled in your quarters, we'll go over things and get started tomorrow. I'm sure you're tired as well." She explained.

"This is going to take some getting used to." Katrina confided in Markus. "I'm so used to doing everything for myself, or you doing it. Will it be scandalous for you to continue assisting me dress when I have two ladies in waiting to attend me?" she asked. "I'm not sure, but let's see what scandalous remarks we can chase up at the next party. I do enjoy dressing and undressing you, my love." He grinned. "Now off with those clothes, we've just a few minutes to change for dinner." They both had to hurry, but managed to make it down to dinner in the allotted fifteen minutes and they were fully dressed, refreshed, and not even breathless. "Whew!" Katrina laughed. "We made it with one second to spare!" Markus laughed as he pulled out her chair. They were actually both ravenous, but neither realized how hungry they really were. Traveling will do that do you, even in a coach.

Anne really knew how to run the affairs at Castle Jamison. She'd had the cook prepare a hearty lamb stew with fresh baked bread. It was filling and really hit the spot. The cook was wonderfully adept with everything she prepared. There were always just the right spices and although it had sat for an hour awaiting their arrival, you could not tell at all. Even Markus commented that it was better than he remembered. They chatted idly over dinner and told Anne she'd done a wonderful job of sprucing up the castle in their absence.

"I have strict instructions to look over the nursery and see what's needed as Markus plans to fill it with lots of babies." Katrina told her. "I am going to go into Manchester to order some clothes and baby things in preparation. We all know what Markus wants, Markus gets." She laughed and so did Anne and Markus. It was a castle full of love and respect. The servants were very respectful and loyal to him and he and Katrina appreciated the quality of staff they had and treated them well so everyone was very happy. There was much joy and love to be found within these walls. "I'd also like to have a small party for all the staff if that's ok with you Markus." She asked. "That's a wonderful idea Katrina. Anne, you can offer suggestions and you ladies can start planning that tomorrow." He said.

"I'm thinking some outdoor events, like croquet and lawn bowling. Maybe some races for the men." Katrina stated. "I just want our home and everyone in it to be as happy as we are, to feel like a part of it all, not just a worker, and I want them to be excited and celebrate our union with us. No one here got to celebrate with us at the wedding, so it's a good time to celebrate now that we're back home, before we start having babies and fulfilling our royal duties at court." She added. "Start thinking of other ideas you may have Anne, and we'll discuss it at tea tomorrow. We'll include Lady Penelope and Lady Alicia to help as well, so they feel a welcome part of Castle Jamison." Katrina instructed. "You think of everything my love." Markus said as he leaned over to kiss her. "We are going to be as down to earth as we can be when we rule this kingdom. The people are who support us and as their leaders we need to let them know we appreciate it." He added. "And there's no better place to start than home."

When dinner was finished they did retire and were so tired from the trip, they merely molded themselves against each other and held on tightly for the remainder of the night. They slept soundly and were totally refreshed the next morning.

Upon awakening, they talked a while then started getting dressed for breakfast. They both had a big day. They'd been gone so long, Markus needed to check on everything around the estate to be sure it was all kept in order in his absence. Katrina had a party to plan for the staff. They had a wonderful breakfast and started on their duties. Katrina headed straight for the nursery to see what would be needed when she went into Manchester. All the furniture was in place, so clothes and linens were really all she'd need, and a nice pillow for the rocking chair, so she'd be comfortable feeding the babies. She even liked the color they'd painted it.

Anne had unpacked all her clothes while she and Markus had breakfast. She checked her wardrobe again and decided all she needed was gowns designed for carrying babies; not the tight cinch-waist gowns she currently had. She ran her hand over her flat stomach and really couldn't imagine how she would look with a baby in there.

When she finished, she made her way downstairs to the parlor for tea. All three ladies were waiting when she walked in. The two young ladies were learning already to always be waiting for the mistress, and to never make her wait for you. "Please sit down, let's fix our tea and get started with plans. Alicia I'd like you to take the notes of everything we'll need to prepare, another list of what we'll need to purchase when in town, and a list of all the activities we decide we'll participate in. Now, I've already mentioned a few things I think we could do, so please give me your thoughts and we'll all decide what we like and get it all pulled together." She said.

They decided on croquet, lawn bowling, races and a dance after lunch. Everyone could dance with her and Markus along with their spouses and friends. Some group dances to get everyone started would be nice. They'd have picnic food, sandwiches, vegetables, other side dishes and assorted desserts. They'd have tables set up in one long row so everyone ate together at the same table. They'd also have some couches and chairs set around for those who wanted to watch, or rest from their games. There was a local group of musicians they could hire for the music and Cook could hire some help from the local tavern to assist in preparing everything in advance that could be and for serving so she could participate in everything as well. She was going to invite her uncle and everyone else could invite their family if they had any close who would like to come. Anne would just need a final count of who was going to be attending so she could make sure we had enough seating and food for everyone. They laughed and talked for a couple hours over their tea. They were all four satisfied they'd covered everything and how it would all take place. It was going to be in two weeks, so they had a lot to take care of beforehand. They were all excited; and when the word got out later that morning, the whole place was abuzz. Everyone was looking forward to the party and having a good time.

They'd never done anything like this before; of course they'd never had a celebration like this before either. It had just been Master Markus living there and although there were visitors from time to time, things had really changed since Katrina had come. First her big engagement party to introduce her to the Lords and Ladies, now a party for the servants. This type party was truly unheard of. They already loved Markus, and Katrina had just soared to the top of their lists. He'd always been good to them, fair and just, but he'd never done anything like this to show his gratitude and appreciation for all their hard work, loyalty, and support.

Katrina filled Markus in on the plans as they were getting ready for dinner. Markus knew his wife was one of a kind and would be an amazing queen. She could draw people together who didn't know they were apart. Everyone loved her. He knew this country would be stronger than ever and could learn to work together and he had no doubts they'd survive under his leadership with Katrina by his side. It was going to be an amazing reign.

In the two weeks leading up to the party, everyone settled into their own routine. Markus had rounds to make and things to check out and give his approvals for fixing or replacing to keep things moving. Planting season was at hand so he had to oversee that. They were rotating crops this year and he wanted to be sure things got planted where they needed to be, so he was out most of the day and would come home tired, in time for dinner. He always had time for Katrina though. They'd have their bubble baths together, talk about their day and most evenings fall asleep after making love.

The ladies had made a couple trips to town to secure everything they needed for the party. Katrina had decided to postpone her trip to the dressmakers until after the party when things calmed down and were back to normal. Everyone was so excited and rushing around gathering up stuff and cleaning more, getting the tack cleaned and the horses shoed so everything would be ready for the races. You'd think it were the Queen's ball, with all the scurrying around.

Katrina did manage to take Markus his lunch a few times during those two weeks, so she could spend a few minutes with him during the day. He seemed to come alive, when he saw her coming instead of Henry. She loved that. She knew he truly loved her and always would.

Finally the day arrived and the party was here. It was a beautiful day for it, the sun was shining, the birds were singing and the lawn was immaculate. The servants were putting everything together with a joy in their hearts. They were working, but it was for their benefit. Markus and Katrina were right in there, sleeves rolled up, helping side by side. That made every single person feel good and know they were appreciated, not just as a worker, but a part of Castle Jamison. They started with a croquet tournament and lawn bowling tournament, each set played and the winners from those games moved on till they were down to the final four. They enjoyed lunch and the last games were played. Katrina made it to the semi-final, but was eliminated there. Markus was in the semi-final for the lawn bowling. They were both good sports when they lost and congratulated the victors heartily when it happened. Katrina had even sneaked and had ribbons made for the winners. She and Markus presented them at the end of the tournaments. Now it was time for the horse racing, then dancing. The stable boy won the horse race. The men laughed and said he threatened the horses. If they didn't win when he was riding--no food for a week! Everyone got a big laugh out of that. It was all in good fun and he loved his winner's ribbon.

The musicians began to play a rousing number and Markus shouted "Off to the dance floor!" It was constructed pretty well by the butler. He'd used some lumber they kept on hand for repairs. He'd chosen the straightest and widest boards and laid out a good size floor as well. There was a nice level spot near the front entrance, so that's where he put it. It worked out really well and everyone complemented him on his handiwork. It really did take everyone working together to make it happen so smoothly and with so much revelry.

Markus had grasped Katrina's hand and was the first on the dance floor. He knew it would probably be the last time he'd get to dance with her that evening. Every man there would want to dance with the princess. He would have his fair share of dances as well. When that dance was over, they did a group dance where partners would be changed throughout the dance and different patterns and movements would be completed by everyone. It sort of got everyone up and moving so no one felt strange about dancing, or left out if they had no partner to dance with. Katrina danced about 10 dances before excusing herself to get something to drink and a bite of food. There would be no formal dinner, just foods people could snack on whenever they got hungry. There was plenty to go around though. She took a fifteen minute break and was right back to dancing. During her break, she chatted a little with her uncle and a few of the other older family members that had come to participate in the event. Everyone she spoke to said they were having a wonderful time and extended their thanks for going to so much trouble for them. "Without all of you, Markus and I wouldn't be able to function as well and do the things we do. We appreciate everyone and what every single person does for us to keep this place going. We are concerned about all of you and hope we can stay a close knit group for many many years." She told them.

Just when her uncle thought she couldn't make him any prouder, she'd turn around and do something like this. She'd never have to ask twice or raise her voice to any of the staff for the rest of her life. They were as devoted to her as he and Markus were and she didn't even do it for that. She did it because it was the right thing to do and Markus was just the same kind of guy. No wonder they were a perfect match!

"I love you more today than I did yesterday." Markus told her as they got ready for bed. "You are truly an amazing woman, my love. You have endeared yourself to our staff and had a splendid time doing it. Every Lord and Lady could take a lesson or two from you. You make me so proud." He said as he kissed her hand, then moved on up her arm finally to her lips. "I truly like every one of them I've met and it's just the right thing to do and I had so much fun doing it!" She said. "I love you more every day my dear." She told him with a kiss.

Chapter 5 – Alexander

When they awoke the next morning, they laid in bed talking for a while about what a great party it was and about their future. "I think we're on the right track, my love." He said with a smile. "We know our priorities and we agree on them. We both want the best for each other and our country. We are a perfect match." He told her.

"Markus, I have something I've been thinking about and would like to discuss with you." She began. "Of course my love, what is it?" he asked. "Alexander, she replied. "I just can't help thinking about him. I just feel so sorry for him. He really is a victim and had he had someone to really care for him, he might have listened and not become so bitter." She added. "What do you have in mind?" Markus asked. "With your permission, of course, I'd like to send him a letter every month. Just telling him about things in the kingdom, sharing the fact that he's not forgotten and we'd like to have a relationship with him. I'd also like to send him something to read or something to do so his mind has something to concentrate on besides revenge." She spoke quietly as she looked into Markus' eyes. "I understand." He told her. I feel the same way, but I'm afraid a letter directly from me would just fuel his anger."

"I think it would be a great thing for you to do.

I think we can arrange one book at a time to be delivered and exchanged. I don't think he can cause any trouble with one book. I don't think we could send him paint, or even a pencil and paper, he's smart and good with stuff, he'd probably build a weapon from a pencil or paint brush, hurt someone and escape. Do you have any other ideas?" he asked. "Well I was thinking if he wanted to send a letter to anyone, we could get the captain to write it for him. If he's there and has a lot of contact, Alexander may actually decide to ask him a question or two about what happened. I also thought that we could give him chalk. I don't think it could be used as a weapon, but he could draw with it on paper or even on the walls of his cell. I just think he's family and well I just hate him being mistreated, even after all he put us through." She finished.

"See, this is why I love you so much, your heart is so big and forgiving. He terrified you so much with his actions, but you still care for him." He began. "If you remember darling, you also terrified me much with your actions and I totally forgave you all that and surrendered my everything to you, for you to do with as you wish." She inserted. "You are correct there and I do apologize again for the times you were scared. I'll inform the guard and instruct them the captain will be visiting and may even be taking letters from Alexander to deliver or dispatch to whomever he wishes to write. The captain will have to use much discretion should Alexander try to give hidden meaning in his letters. We'd hate to help him start the next revolt. I'll also contact the captain and ask this favor of him and instruct him to be candid with Alexander and answer honestly whatever questions he may have." Markus finished. "Oh sweetheart, I do thank you. If we can build even a little good will with him, it will be a start and I won't feel nearly as bad with him in prison if we afford him these tiny luxuries." She hugged Markus as she spoke. She really did wish him well, and Markus missed him terribly.

Markus said he would write the letters to the captain and to the guard that evening and dispatch with her letter tomorrow. Later that morning after breakfast, Katrina sat down to write to Alexander. She had so much she wanted to say, but had to be careful of how she worded everything, so she wrote this:

        "Dearest Alexander, we wanted to send you some reading material and chalk so you could draw if you'd like. Also Markus arranged for the captain to come by in case you'd like to dictate a letter to anyone. He'll be happy to do that for you and will dispatch them as soon as you dictate. Whenever you finish with the book, they'll trade it out for another. If you have any preferences, please tell the guard. There's a lot of things you can't have in prison, but we know you're going stir crazy with nothing to do. You're just not the kind of man to sit around staring at four walls and not go crazy.

I want you to know that while I was really scared most of the time, I did enjoy much of our time together. I wish it had not been under those circumstances but you do have a good heart and are funny and attentive. I think if you can get past everything, you could find a wonderful woman and have a very satisfying life. You are so much like Markus in many ways and I know you must miss him as much as he misses you. You were like brothers you know. I'd like to write you monthly, but if you don't want me to, just send word and I won't write. I only hope to cheer you somewhat, but never to annoy or be a burden to you. Let me know your wishes. Your cousin, Princess Katrina"

Markus thought it was perfect. He drafted his two letters ready for dispatch; adding the needed money for the gifts. "I hope you can soften his heart my love." Markus told Katrina. "So do I. I so wish we could have him as part of our family, our real family, not just a relative in jail who hates us." She explained. "Maybe you should send your mother a note explaining our plans, just in case something would come up, she'd be aware." She added. "Good thinking my love." Markus leaned over, kissed her and said "I'll definitely do that too."

Chapter 6 - What a surprise!

"Now I'll be gone in the morning before you arise. I have to go to the farthest farm on our estate to check it and consult with the shareholder. I'm taking Henry with me, so Sully will drive you into town. He's not as crisp as Henry, but he'll do and he knows the horses and coach. You ladies enjoy your shopping. Make sure you get girly things for the baby. I know our first is going to be a little princess." He smiled. "I'm ordering both girl and boy things as we don't know for sure what our baby will be, when we have one." She informed him. "Have it your way, but the boy things can wait." He added. "Oh Markus, I do love your persistence, even with things you can't control." She laughed and then moved in for a kiss. "It's supposed to be a beautiful day, so I think I'll send Sully on to see if Uncle can join me for lunch while we shop and place my orders. I also think I'll see if Lady Penelope wants to invite her mother or sister to join her. Lady Alicia can dine with Sully." She continued. "I think that's a splendid plan." Markus was enthused about her trip. "Tell him to come visit for a week or two when he can get away. I owe him a lot. He kept you safe till you were old enough for me to marry you. I'll forever be grateful." He finished.

Katrina was up early. She decided to spend two nights at her uncle's. She wrote Markus a note and informed Anne to pack her a bag for an extra night and to let Sully know. She then told Ladies Penelope and Alicia to ready their things. If Lady Penelope would like to stay with her family, that would be quite all right. Katrina wanted to visit her father's grave while she was so close. If she became with child, she would not be able to travel and it could be a long time before she was close again. It was a two day journey to Manchester so they'd stay at an inn going and coming, but staying with her uncle two nights would give her plenty of time to do her shopping and errands, spend a little time with him and visit the graveyard. They'd also have time to rest a little before heading home. They ate early and were off. Cook had prepared lunches for them to have along the way. Dinner would be at the Inn and the tavern cook would prepare them lunches for the next day's travel.

The ladies were so excited. They chatted about the house party they'd just had and then moved on to the upcoming shopping and Lady Penelope's visit with her family. They both wanted to know about Katrina's family, so she filled them in. They were sad for her, but so happy it had turned out good in the end for her and Master Markus. They both thought they were the perfect match and would make great rulers and beautiful babies. They both told Katrina a little about their families and the day passed pretty quickly. They were almost at the inn before conversation even started to slow down.

They had a good dinner and hurried on to hot baths and bed. They'd been so engaged in conversation, they truly didn't realize how tired they were, and how many sore spots they had from the long ride.

They all slept very well and were totally refreshed the next morning. They dressed, had a delicious breakfast, and left for Manchester. It would be a pretty long day, but they'd arrive late afternoon and have a while before dinner to stretch their legs and enjoy the sunshine. Her uncle was so happy to see her. "I wasn't expecting you!" he exclaimed. "I know." she said, "but I was coming to see the dressmaker, shoemaker and do a few other things and I wanted to see you and visit father's grave while I was here; so we're taking our time and making a longer stay of it." She smiled "Of course if we soon have a baby on the way, I don't know how long it will be before I can come back, so I figured I'd better take advantage of this trip." She added. "Well I'm glad you did!" he exclaimed as he hugged her tight and guided her into the house. "I pray you will have one soon, you both are so alive and happy with each other, a baby would fit in so nicely and be a very welcome addition to your family. Got to keep those heirs coming!" He winked.

It was short notice, but dinner was amazing. Lady Penelope did stay with her family but Lady Alicia had dinner with Katrina and her uncle. She was very pleasant company. Katrina liked her, but didn't seem to have the same connection that she had with Penelope. Probably because they had lived in different towns. She made herself a mental note to get to know her a little better and work on the compatibility that she shared with Penelope. It must be hard to leave home and basically live with strangers. She'd seen and met the royal family, but had not really conversed with them. Katrina pulled her into the conversation every time she found an opportunity, and found she was really warming up to her. When they had children, her ladies would need to assist some with them and she wanted to be sure she had their confidence and loyalty to her children, as much as to her and Markus. There would be a nanny on staff, but sometimes she would need assistance and Alicia would probably be the one to take on those jobs.

Katrina had already noticed that Alicia and Penelope had developed a bond and were becoming fast friends. She'd also noted Sully was quite taken with the task of coach driver and footman. It was a nice promotion for him that could become permanent as time passed and they had more occasions for his services as such. It was good to see everyone growing and coming together to work for the whole.

They arose early to dress, have breakfast and head into town for shopping. First and most important was the dressmakers. She had things ready that Katrina had ordered before.

She measured Katrina's waist and told her she was with child. "I'm barely ½ an inch bigger", she exclaimed. "Why do you think I'm with child?" she asked. "You glow Your Highness and this particular spot will gain about this much. The lower belly will get much bigger. I'd better get very busy designing and making your new gowns and undergarments. You're going to need them very quickly. Be sure to get some flat shoes, it will be more comfortable for you near the end. When I finish your gowns, I'll start the clothes for your little girl." "How do you know it's a girl?" Katrina interrupted. "If I measure this part right here around your hips, it will tell me, but I know your body so well, I can already tell. It will be about ½ inch smaller right here. Let me measure and we'll see." She looped the tape around Katrina at that exact spot and sure enough she was just a little smaller. "I've only been wrong once My Lady, but there's always a chance I could be again." She finished. "No, you're probably right, do mine, girl's clothes, then boy's clothes. The Prince assured me the first would be a girl, then I was to have 3-4 boys before I could have another girl. I guess he knows too." Katrina smiled. "I can't even tell a difference in my body yet. Let me pick some material and look at some of your sketches and we'll be finished."

Katrina picked several designs she liked for boys and girls. She picked several fabrics for all three and a couple to match hers. "Thanks so much, I can hardly wait for everything to arrive." Katrina told her, then added "Please don't advertise the baby yet. I'd like to see the doctor and let Markus know first. We'll send an announcement out to all the land." Katrina hugged her and left for the shoemaker's.

She told him they were planning a family and would need shoes for that time. He had a few designs to choose from that would allow breathing room for swelling and low heals to ease the back pain. She ordered two pair, one for dress and one for day. Now to shop for linens.

Katrina chose several pieces in white, a blanket in every color to complement the material she'd chosen at the dressmaker's, some booties, hats and then the linens for the nursery, diapers, oh and a lovely pillow set for the rocking chair in the nursery. She also got a small footstool for that room as well so if she needed to prop her feet up, she'd be equipped. They had lunch at an outside table. It was a beautiful day and Katrina daydreamed about the baby that might be growing inside. So with that thought in mind, Katrina went to the jewelers and ordered a tiny pearl bracelet for

*her new daughter. They wondered through the
entire town and at least stopped in every store
to look around, even if they didn't find
something they wanted to purchase. They
found a few things they thought they needed.
She stopped by the flower stand and picked up
a nice bouquet for her father's grave and
headed to her uncle's.*

*She found him in his study. "Uncle I have the
best secret to tell you." She began. "You mean
about the baby?" he asked. "How is it I'm the
last to know?" she exclaimed. "I've just seen
that glow from your mother and my wife." He
answered. "Turn around." Katrina turned
sideways. "Yep, it's a girl too." He added.
"That's exactly what the dressmaker said. I
can't believe you both know and I had no clue!"
Katrina sounded amazed and she was. Surely
they were guessing. "I wonder if Markus
knows somehow?" she pondered "He hasn't said
anything, so I'm guessing not. "He's young and
may not have witnessed the beauty of a
woman with child." Her uncle stated. "You'll
probably get to tell him." He added. "I hope I
get to tell someone!" Katrina exclaimed. This
just wasn't fair, she should know first.*

*"I'm going to the graveyard to visit the
graves." Katrina told him. I'll be back for
dinner." She added. Katrina took her time
strolling among the beautiful flowers along the
path, enjoying the sunshine on her back. She*

wanted to take everything in as she was sure she wouldn't be able to come back soon. She thought of her family often, so it wasn't like she would forget them, but coming here seemed to connect her more. She knew they weren't here, this was just the place the body was kept; but still it seemed to be the spot she could commune with them. She would always tell them about her life, her hopes, dreams, and whatever was bothering her. She really didn't think they could hear her, but saying things out loud helped her to get a handle on her feelings and help her decide any decisions she needed to make. When she arrived, she placed the bouquet just perfectly on her father's grave, said hello to them all and began to fill them in on her life. She was gushing with love when she spoke about Markus. She shared her fears and concerns about giving birth and then her excitement about having a child and what if they were right? What if it were a little girl? She could see what a bond she'd share with her and how beautiful she'd be and how much her daddy would adore her. These thoughts chased away her fears and besides, she had the most experienced mid-wife there was in the kingdom ready and excited to be there for the birth. Katrina talked about two hours and when she'd worked out all her feelings and felt comfortable with her decisions, she said good-bye and headed back to her uncle's.

They would be leaving in the morning on their

two day journey back home and Katrina wanted to spend as much time with her uncle as she could. She also must remember to tell him how much Markus looked forward to his visit as well. He was standing in the doorway as she came up the walk. "I figured it was just about time for you to get back and I know it may be your last trip here for a while, so I thought I'd catch you so we can spend a little time together before dinner. I miss you my child." He said as he hugged her close. They joined arms and walked to his study. Katrina loved it in there, it was always warm and cozy. She'd curl up on the settee and sometimes fall asleep there while he worked. It was a safe place and it smelled like her uncle. She liked that and was always comforted there. "Perfect!" she exclaimed. "I miss you too uncle, that's why I wanted to spend extra time with you too. I was going to look you up when I got back." She laughed. "Great minds." He said.

They really didn't have anything to discuss, they just needed to be together. They talked about the past, the fun they'd enjoyed, her sixteenth birthday party, Markus, the new baby on the way, her life at Castle Jamison, what he was up to and that she worried if he was happy since she was gone, him being all alone again. He assured her he was and had actually been thinking of doing some courting in the future. He wasn't quite ready, but had given it some thought. She told him they wanted him to come visit soon and if he did start courting, he'd better be sending her letters to keep her informed. She was beginning to sound like a parent already she thought. They talked till dinner time and were still laughing when they went in.

Lady Penelope had returned since they were leaving so early the next morning, she felt she'd better stay here so as not to cause any delays. She brought a beautiful pink dressing gown for Katrina's first girl Penelope beamed as she told of her mother making it, hoping that Katrina would like it and allow her first daughter to wear it. She also did the needlework picture on the chest. It was the word princess with tiny little flowers around it. It was so detailed and delicate, Katrina was thrilled. "What an amazing detail and such a heartfelt gift!" Katrina exclaimed. "Oh I do love it and I shall send your mother a thank you before I leave." she continued. After dinner, Katrina did just that too. She prepared a very formal thank you letter on the royal stationery and wrote a nice note and gave it to her uncle to dispatch the next morning. He told her to expect many more things like this from her subjects. She was loved by all and they'd all want to participate, any way they could, in the royal activities and especially the birth of a baby!

They retired for the evening and Katrina slept

soundly and dreamed of a beautiful little baby growing silently in her belly. Markus would be elated. He could hardly wait to be a father and Katrina could not be happier either. It seems her life of tragedy was now a charmed existence and they were on top of the world!

After a very filling breakfast, and assurances the lunch they were taking would be amazing, they were off. She and the ladies were back to their usual chit chat in minutes. Lady Penelope pointed out many sites to Lady Alicia and what she didn't know about or who she didn't know, Katrina filled in for them both. It was a beautiful day and a very pleasant journey. They stretched their legs a good bit and enjoyed their lunch, which, true to reports, was amazing; but didn't linger too long as they all were ready to go home. The rest of the trip was pretty uneventful, just beautiful countryside and a good night's sleep at the tavern.

They arrived home just after lunch. They hadn't had anything prepared for them as they really didn't want to stop. Sully made excellent time as the ladies only had to make one quick stop along the way and they hurried then, made two laps around the coach and horses and were back inside refreshed and ready to go. Katrina knew cook would have something she could serve them within minutes and she was right.

They were barely in the house, when Markus rode up. He practically ran in the house, grabbed Katrina and kissed her passionately twice before letting her go. "Markus, there are ladies present." She exclaimed rather breathlessly. "Well, they'll have to get used to seeing me affectionate with my wife." He said. "I love you so much, I just can't help myself. It's been days since I've seen you." He smiled and kissed her again and then took her arm and urged her upstairs to freshen up a little. "Lady Penelope, would you have Anne bring Katrina's lunch up to the sitting room, she can freshen up and have her lunch up there with me, so we can talk." He asked over his shoulder. "Of course Your Highness." She said quickly as they were almost out of sight.

Markus helped her out of her gown, it wasn't too dusty from the trip; and she washed her face and hands, then slipped into a comfortable, no frills, day gown. She felt very refreshed and was just finishing when Anne brought in her lunch. "I'm starved!" Katrina exclaimed and quickly began to enjoy her lunch. It was splendid. She had braised quail, roasted potatoes, carrots, a hot biscuit and a slice of apple pie.

When she'd finished, they really got down to some conversation. She filled him in on their trip, the shopping and even her visit to the graveyard. She did, however leave till last the dressmaker's and her uncle's comments about a baby, and the adorable gown Lady Penelope's mother had sewn as a gift for the new princess.

Markus was on cloud nine when he heard their remarks and saw the beautiful little gown. "I told you!" He exclaimed. "I told you." "Markus, calm down just a little. I can't even tell yet and I haven't seen a doctor or even a mid-wife, so let's don't get too excited. Plus we won't really know until the baby is born if it's a boy or a girl. I don't want you to get your hopes up too high, or too early." She warned. "OK, he conceded, I'll do my best to contain myself until you know, then I'm telling the world!" he exclaimed. "Katrina you've made me happier than I was before and I didn't think that was possible! I love you so much! We're going to be wonderful parents. I knew it would be a girl too. I told you." Katrina knew there was no calming him down. "I should know for sure in two weeks. Do you think you can contain yourself until then? I'd hate for your mother to hear it from someone other than us." She explained. "You're right my love, as always. It will be our secret and we'll plan a trip to the palace in a fortnight so we can tell Mother." He grinned and then added "Because I know it is true and I'm thrilled!"

Chapter 7 - An Artist is Born

Alexander ranted and raved for hours when he received the package from Katrina. He'd look at it and get mad again. He'd read the letter and get mad again. He couldn't understand how these people thought he could or would have a relationship with them. He would never "get past everything" and move on with his life until he became ruler. When he finally calmed down much later the next day, the book caught his eye. He picked it up and laid it down. It was like admitting he was wrong if he accepted anything from them. He would like something to do, of that Katrina was very correct. He'd nearly lost his mind. He couldn't imagine being like this for years. He started to read. He actually only stopped for his meal and then went right back to reading. He had nothing else to do, so he kept reading. He finished it in two days and it was a rather large book. When they brought his dinner the second day, the guard had another book with him. "I noticed you were almost finished so I took the liberty of securing another for you." He smiled.

If there's anything special you'd like to read, let me know. I just picked one that looked good." "Thanks Alexander said as he slid the first book out and accepted the new book. He ate, read a while then glanced over at the chalk. Maybe he would look at it and see if he could still draw. He was pretty good as a child. Maybe with practice, he'd do alright. He was actually still pretty good. He drew a picture on the paper that came with the book, then looked around his cell. He actually smiled for the first time since being imprisoned. He took his chalk and started in the corner of his cell closest to his bed. He outlined a picture on every wall, concluding where he started, with the exception of the floor and ceiling. He was almost out of chalk. Just outlining used up all he had. He called out to the guard and asked if he was allowed more. The guard said as far as he knew, since he was allowed to have it, and no one said that's all he could have, so yes he could have it. It was obvious there was little or none left. "When the second guard arrives, I'll go fetch you some more." He declared.

When he returned with more chalk, Alexander immediately began to fill in his drawings. He shaded and colored as much as he had chalk to do, then asked for more. The next morning at the changing of the guard, the one leaving would first go and fetch some more chalk before going home, and some more paper too. He was not allowed a pen as he could use it as a weapon. He drew a picture for Katrina. It was a picture of her on horseback riding across a meadow with mountains in the background and the palace in the distance. She was wearing a beautiful gown which flowed out as she was riding. She had a crown on her

head and a smile on her face. It looked just like
her, and he was quite pleased with himself as
he looked at it. He asked the guard to have the
captain come he wanted to send Lady Katrina
a letter.

While he waited for the guard to come, before
he started reading, Alexander decided he was
not mad at Katrina, he actually liked her a lot
and under different circumstances, would have
been a contender for her hand in marriage.
He would have fought tooth and nail to have
her as his bride. Normally he'd get mad
thinking about what Markus had that he
should have had instead, but this time, he knew
Katrina and Markus loved each other and
with the ordeal he'd put them through, their
love had become much stronger and would
never be broken. She was his and there was no
changing that. He resigned himself to the fact
that she was his cousin and it looked like she
may be his friend as well. He was truly
grateful for the friendship she had shown him
with company, books and chalk. His mind was
not wasting away and tormenting him with
unfilled time on his hands. He still exercised in
his cell daily to keep his muscles loose and
strong. He didn't know if he'd need them for
another battle, a war, or just to take care of
himself, but he knew he would not allow
himself to just waste away to nothing in this
prison. When the captain arrived, Alexander
was reading his new book as he'd run out of

chalk and was waiting for more to be delivered. The captain asked if he wanted to hear about his father and he immediately said "I do not want to hear any of your lies!" The captain told him whenever he wanted to hear what happened, just let him know. He would not tell him any lies, just what happened to so many men that day. "I was in such a good mood before you came and started that nonsense." Alexander told him and then added. "Now, just don't talk to me and simply write the letter for which you've been instructed to come." He dictated:

"My dearest Katrina, I appreciate your kindness and understanding of the agony I have been experiencing as a captive in this prison. I am a man of action and it's extremely hard to be secluded here. I am stretching and getting as much exercise as I can. That's really all there is to do except think. I would like to say my meals are adequate and I am given bathing privileges, so my health is very good. The books and chalk have been more than a comfort to me. I believe you have saved my life and for that I will always be in your debt. I have drawn a picture of you in chalk and have enclosed it with this letter. I do hope you enjoy it. I have also drawn much on the walls of my cell. It is a comfort to me to do the work and to have something to look at other than gray walls. I very much would like to converse with you monthly as you suggest, but more often than that would be a welcome reprieve as I struggle to maintain sanity in this place. I am sorry for any pain or discomfort I caused you and especially any fear you had for your safety. I would never hurt you. You have my word that I will always be your champion. It is my heart's desire to have a life with a woman like you some day with children and laughter to fill my ears and freedom to enjoy it all. Again, I thank you and will always remain your loyal servant." Alexander

When the captain finished, Alexander handed him the drawing and told him to send this to her as well. "May I look?" the captain asked. "I suppose." Alexander told him. "Oh my, you have truly captured her spirit as well as her beauty. You are indeed a wonderful artist Alexander." He finished. "Just leave me and have it sent to her." Alexander told him rather gruffly. "I have a book to read."

The captain did just that and Alexander went back to his book, but decided he'd draw her face on the ceiling above his bed, so he could look at her as he lay there doing nothing else.

Katrina was sitting in the garden, waiting for Markus to finish a few things before going with him for a ride, when her packet arrived. She quickly opened it and on top was her portrait. It was amazing. Such detail in chalk, she could only imagine his skill with paint and a brush.

She had just finished reading the letter when Markus came up. "What do you have there, my love?" he asked as he sat down beside her. "It's a letter from Alexander and a portrait of me." She said as she handed them both over for Markus to look at and read. "Well at least I don't have to worry about your safety any further. He made no mention of me, which is a good sign as he could have lashed out instead of remaining quiet. There is even a mention of a happy life, but I fear that is to cover his longing to be with you. I think it was a good idea to give him something to do. He does have a great talent for drawing. I wish I could trust him with paint and brushes. I wish I could trust him to behave and not be a threat to our kingdom. I would love to be able to let him out of prison, but as it is, it's just not possible." He finished with quite a sad look on his face.

"We'll keep sending letters and keep him supplied with chalk and paper to keep his mind occupied with something other than plotting against you and your mother. Maybe there will come a time we feel it safe to give him other things. We are doing the right thing, Markus. We have to show him he's still our family and we love him. He just can't be free as he won't accept the facts of his father's death, and his lack of a claim to the throne. I think he'll come around one day. "She said with a smile on her face and she leaned over for a kiss as she finished speaking. "I love you so much, my darling. I do wish he could be as happy as we are." She told him. "I don't think there's a man on this planet that can be as happy as me." Markus told her as he kissed her again. "Now let's go for that ride before I take you back upstairs." He smiled as he took her hand and lifted her up. "You won't be able to ride in a few more months, so you'd better take advantage of it now. We'll have to be extra careful with you and our little princess. We can't have you both falling off a horse or anything. You are both too precious to me for that. We should think of a name for her." Katrina interrupted with "I have. You told me we had to incorporate mother's name into our daughter's but I think it should be pretty prominent. I have been thinking about Anne Marie. I'd also like to call her by both names as that's your mother and my mother always with us both. Do you like it?" she asked. "I love it!" Markus exploded and picked her up and twirled her around. It's a beautiful name and goes well with princess too." He added. "Well Katrina and Anne Marie, shall we go for a ride?" he asked. "Of course we will, silly. After all we both love you dearly." She added with the most beautiful smile.

When they returned from their ride, they talked more about the baby and wondered if Nanny Gertrude would still be alive to deliver their fourth generation into this world. They *were both confident she was a tough old bird and although she may just be an advisor versus totally hands on, her expertise would be appreciated. They talked a little more about Alexander and if there would ever be a hope of changing his mind. He had still refused to talk to the captain about that day. It was truly a shame things had happened as they did. Markus held her in his lap as they talked and gently rubbed his hand over her stomach. My little girl is in there, he'd say and it seemed like beams of sunshine literally shot from his face. He was beaming and so proud. If he got this happy and excited now, imagine how he'd be when he held little Anne Marie in his arms.*

They spent many hours in each other's arms just like they were right now, during the next two weeks awaiting the announcement of Princess Anne Marie.

Finally the day was here, the doctor came and examined Katrina and confirmed she was indeed carrying a royal baby. He gave her some instructions and Markus listened as though his life depended on it. He would make sure Katrina did everything she was supposed to do and nothing she was instructed not to do. They both were terribly excited and could hardly wait to leave for the palace and tell the queen. They decided to stay a couple weeks so they could have a long visit since they would not be able to travel as Katrina got closer to the time. It would also give him a chance to go to the prison and attempt to talk to Alexander again. Hopefully he would be more agreeable to a visit since Katrina had written to him a couple times and they'd given him books, chalk and paper to occupy his mind and fill his time.

The queen was elated and immediately sent the trumpeters out to make the announcement. She couldn't wait to have grandchildren. She'd been waiting for quite some time, but was so glad that it was Katrina who was giving them to her and not some bride she'd chosen for Markus. They were a good pairing and if it were possible, Katrina had gotten more beautiful since they'd last been together.

It was fun to be at the palace. There was always so much activity going on with lunches, dinners, dances, dignitaries visiting and just the bustle of so many servants coming and going. Compared, Castle Jamison didn't even seem like a royal residence at all. Katrina and Markus thoroughly enjoyed themselves every minute they were there. It didn't leave them a lot of alone time, but they made up for that every night in their room. Markus really didn't know how he could love her any more, but he did and he wanted her to know it too. They had been there for almost a week before Markus decided he'd go and see Alexander. He was looking forward to seeing him, again, but knew it would probably be a major fight once he got there. He still mourned the loss of their friendship and retained a glimmer of hope that it could one day be restored.

Markus walked quietly up to the bars of Alexander's cell and stood marveling at the beauty on the walls. It was like standing inside a painting. There was lush green hills and valleys, a beautiful waterfall in the midst of a stream. The skies were full of big puffy clouds and there was a forest with a log cabin near the front. There were numerous types of flowers, a castle in the distance and a quaint little village at the far end. He'd drawn the blacksmith's shop with horses tied in the front. There was a pastry shop and dressmakers with exquisite gowns hanging in the window. A sundry store and several other buildings drawn in perfect proportions, children were playing in that creek and there were deer in the field. There were people at a street fair and Alexander and Katrina holding hands in the middle of one of the streets. Markus was so enthralled in its beauty, he didn't even realize Alexander had come over to stand near him inside the cell. As a matter of fact, he actually jumped when Alexander spoke. "I see you are enjoying your lovely bride's portrait over at the street fair. She is exquisite, don't you think?" Alexander asked with a smile on his face. "She is." Markus spoke "If only she were with her husband instead of you." He finished. "Don't get all riled up, I'm drawing pictures of *things I remember and make me happy. I was very happy posing as you, with her at my side. You are a very lucky man, Markus." He finished.*

"I am indebted to her, well both of you, it seems. I truly was losing my mind and now I actually look at this and smile. I wish she could come and see it. Do you think that's possible?" He asked. Markus hesitated for a minute before answering. "I think we'd both like spending some time with you. I miss you terribly and we'd both like us to be family, if that's ever possible." He finished. "She can be my family any time." Alexander began "She had no part in any of this." Markus interrupted him by saying "I had no part either. Your father was dead, my mother was the queen and I am in line for the throne. None of that, nor anything leading up to it was of my doing, yet you would have killed me had your plan not been detected." "How can you expect me to get over that or undo any of it. I've tried to get you to talk to the captain and you refuse. Your father was sick, along with many others in that army." "Stop it!" Alexander cut him off. "I'll be civil and talk to you if it means I can talk to her, but I won't listen to any of that nonsense about my father." He stated as he crossed his arms over his chest. "So, you still plan on killing me and my mother so you can have the throne?" Markus asked. "Honestly, I really don't have a

plan for anything. There's nothing I can do in here, so there's no need to think about any plans for anything in my life." I would not take your life Markus. I owe that much to Katrina; but as far as your mother, I'm undecided on that at the moment. I try not to dwell on any of it. I feel so desperate when I do and I don't like that black side to take over my thoughts and actions, so can't we talk about other things? He asked.

The mood was better, lighter. Markus was so thrilled he felt a little safer with him, but still worried about his mother. "Of course we can." Markus answered. I'd like to know what you plan on drawing next and if there's a square inch left in your cell for you to draw on. I would love to give you some oils, canvases, and brushes to work with. Can I have your word you will not try to use the tools to harm anyone or try to escape?" he asked. Alexander actually perked up at the thought. "Yes, you have my word. I would love to do some paintings. Thank you so very much. I appreciate your mercy. I'm sure mine would not have gone so far. I am humbled by your grace. You will truly make a great ruler of this country." He spoke those words with a little wistfulness in his voice. He seemed to be accepting the fact that he would never rule their country. It saddened him, but it no longer made him angry and violent.

Markus thought he needed to bring them back to a lighter tone. "What would you like to do with your paintings? Do you want to do them for particular people, or do you want them sold and if so, what do you want us to do with the money? You could give it to the church, or the orphanage? It's something for you to think about and decide. We can talk about it later after you make your decision. I know Katrina and I would love a few for Castle Jamison. Our room could definitely use a portrait of Katrina like she appears on your wall. You truly captured her inside and out in that one. If you'd do something large for our sitting room and even a scene with baby animals in a field or something appropriate for our nursery, that would be wonderful too."

As soon as Markus finished that sentence, Alexander's head popped up "Is Katrina with child?" He asked. "Yes, we just made the announcement. The baby should come in January, probably around the 20th. Seems like our wedding night was very productive." He said with a smile. "Well, congratulations. Tell her I'm so happy for her, she'll be a wonderful mother. I hope it's a girl that looks just like her." "I said that too!" Markus interrupted. "Then, of course, I want some boys, I explained to her. She laughed and said well I'd better do it right then if I want boys." Alexander and Markus laughed together. It was the first time in many years they had shared that common bond that friends share with one another. "How long are you staying this visit?" he asked. "We're here for two weeks. I'll get you some oils and canvas today. Was there a particular reason you asked?" Markus looked at him as he spoke. "I just figured you wouldn't be making too many visits after she's a little farther along, so I thought I might steal a little more of your time if you both might come and visit." He explained in almost a pleading tone of voice. Markus hated to see him subjected like this. He was a strong man and being in prison would have broken his will had he been subjected to living here with nothing to do, for just a little more time.

He'd have to thank Katrina again for her idea of communication, books, and chalk. Markus answered him quickly "Of course we can come visit. We'll bring lunch with us and share a meal with you. Anything particular you'd like to have?" Alexander looked very surprised at that answer. "I'd really like to have venison stew and pie. Any kind is fine, it would just be such a treat for me. I appreciate your gesture." "Great!" Markus exclaimed, "We'll be here in two days. I'll have to alert the cook and we may have to go hunting. I'm not sure they have any venison left from the winter. We'll get it done. Anything else you'd like?" Markus asked. "No, you're going way out of your way already. That will be a feast and your company will be much appreciated." He answered.

"Alexander, I know you don't really want to talk to the captain, but he's too old for battle and has a lot of free time on his hands these days. Would you mind if he came just to visit and maybe play cards with you? I think you both might enjoy that. I know he feels really needed when he comes to write your letters. What do you think?" Markus asked. "I guess that would be alright. If it doesn't work out, I can always tell him I'd rather not do it anymore." Alexander answered as he thought about how nice it would be to have some company. Someone to talk to about the weather would be a help to his mind. He figured Markus may have ulterior motives about using the captain, but he didn't have to listen to him, so he'd get what he could from the time and stop him if he decided to talk about something he didn't want to hear. "Well, I'd better be getting back. We'll see you day after tomorrow. It was truly good to see you today." Markus said with a smile. "It was good to see you too." Alexander answered. Markus couldn't wait to get back to Katrina and tell her the good news. She was just as excited as he was for Alexander. She was also intrigued to see his paintings and see how he'd captured her likeness. Markus dispatched someone to go get the painting supplies and deliver to Alexander. He spoke with the cook and they did have venison, so he wouldn't have to hunt out of season. Katrina set about gathering the things they'd need for their lunch. She chose a bright table cloth, plates and cups. She also chose a wine to compliment the stew. She was sure Alexander would appreciate that, probably more than the stew. She chose a modest day dress in her favorite blue and decided that a little extra effort and décor, like the tablecloth, would make for a nice luncheon. She found herself trying to forget it was in prison and was hoping the niceties would help Alexander forget for a few minutes as well.

She'd convinced Markus they should eat inside the cell. Since he was convinced Alexander was being truthful when he said he'd not hurt either of them. "I just want him to know and understand we don't like his situation but we still love him and we do have compassion for him." She said as Markus questioned all the frills she was gathering. He agreed too.

They both barely made it through the luncheon and dinner, both their minds were on seeing Alexander. They felt they were making progress and would hopefully change his mind totally. It was such a shame and a waste of a good man. He had such qualities that would be beneficial to their country if they could just convince him he was wanted and needed.

Finally! Those two days had dragged by, but it

was almost lunch time and they had their stuff ready and were very excited to be going to visit Alexander. Katrina had no issues going to the prison or lunching with a traitor. She had more love in her heart for mankind in general and even more for family. Alexander had been just as anxious as they were.

Alexander was pacing his cell. He could barely wait to see them, especially Katrina. He couldn't believe his eyes, when the guard opened his cell door and Markus and Katrina walked in. She gave him a hug first and then Markus did as soon as they set their stuff on the table the guard had carried in. Katrina turned to set the table. She had linens even and wine. Alexander could just stare in disbelief at the things she was placing on the table. He also noticed three chairs were brought in and the cell door was still standing open wide. It took her less than three minutes to get lunch ready to serve. She turned to see them both just standing watching her. "Oh my! You boys haven't even spoken a word. Sit, let's eat and talk." She began. Markus and Alexander both moved to pull out her chair. Alexander stopped short and let Markus have the honor. They then took their chairs on either side of her, and across from each other.

The food smelled wonderful. Katrina handed Markus the wine to open and pour as she dipped out the hearty stew. She passed the pan *of bread around and they began to eat. The conversation was pretty lively considering where they were. It was like friends having lunch in the countryside. She was amazed at the drawings in his cell and especially the likeness of her. "You should put clouds on the ceiling." She said as she looked up, but stopped speaking as she spied the outline of her face above his bed. "I'm sorry, Katrina, I really should not have put that there, but seeing your face keeps me sane. I'm comforted by your smile and the love in your eyes and the joy in your heart. I felt so at ease with you when we were together. It was an easy thing to make myself believe we could be together with Markus out of the picture. Now I just look at your face and see a kind-hearted woman who is strong enough to rule a kingdom and soft enough to make a man turn to jelly. You are a remarkable woman, Katrina, and I admire you for how you handled yourself with me and how you love your husband. Markus, I'll wipe it off if you want me to." He said as quickly as possible as he locked eyes with Markus. "I think it's ok if that's how she makes you feel and it doesn't cause my lady any distress. Also it's imperative you know she is my lady and you looking at her will not instill any feelings that one day she may be yours." He added.*

"I'm past all that now Markus, truly I am. She's a prize for sure, but she's your prize and I owe her so much and you as well. Any other

traitor would have been hanged and shown no mercy. Not only have you shown me mercy, but have saved my sanity and made me a productive person again. I still feel I should be king, but I know that will never be and I do want to keep moving forward and I don't want to lose any more of my family, especially since it's become so beautiful and caring for me."

"Ok then", Katrina spoke. "Let's talk about those clouds." She was an artist in her own right at diffusing situations, changing the subject, and using her charm to lighten any mood and quiet any turmoil. They did talk for several hours before Markus and Katrina decided they really had to go. As they said their goodbyes Alexander asked if she'd stop by before they left and retrieve her painting. He would be working on it starting this evening. She agreed and they gathered their stuff, hugged again and left. Markus instructed the guard to leave the table and a chair.

Alexander did begin immediately on Katrina's portrait. Markus had supplied him with a lot of paint and about twenty different sizes of canvases. He wanted to do it while she was so fresh in his mind. He actually did two before she arrived to pick them up. He did a portrait of her from the shoulders up and he did a full length portrait of her with child. He could only imagine how beautiful she would look with the glow of a child within and he wanted *her to have that to look forward to, so she would only be happy and appreciate the changes in her body and what they meant for her family.*

Katrina came alone and was stunned at how detailed the portraits were. He was definitely a master painter. She cried when she saw the full length one of her with a full belly. It really brought home the reality of what was happening to her. She knew there was a baby there, but it just didn't seem real. Probably because there was no physical changes yet. This showed her a woman she hadn't expected to be quite so soon. It still showed her with a beautiful body, but now with a new presence she hadn't felt yet. She told him they both meant the world to her and she was so grateful he cared so much for her. She and Markus certainly loved and cared for him. "I'll continue to write you, but may not travel until after the baby comes." She told him as she hugged him good-bye. He handed her the portraits and bid her safe journey. She smiled and the guard closed the door behind her. He couldn't have been happier had he been free.

He was anxious to begin his next painting. He already knew what he wanted to paint and she would love it even more. He was going to paint her in a dressing gown, seated in a nice cushy chair with her beautiful daughter on her lap in a nice frilly gown and blanket. It would

show Princess Anne Marie as an almost exact
replica of Katrina. He could see her now,
Katrina's face and Markus' dark hair. She
would be as striking as her mother with her
sapphire eyes staring right out from the
canvas. He also wanted to do something extra
special for Katrina as she had been so kind to
him and he knew how much a baby would
mean to her. She was so full of life, one would
only expect that to spill over into a new life
born of a love he could only hope to come close
to one day when he was no longer a captive.
He had changed and was changing still.
Katrina had done that to him and he was
grateful to her for it. It's like he'd been reborn.
Katrina couldn't wait to show Markus and the
queen the two portraits Alexander had given
her. She also had to get them framed before she
left for home. The queen cried just like
Katrina had and Markus just stood there
looking at it all choked up as the realization hit
him like it had overtaken Katrina. "I hadn't
imagined you looking like that yet. I suppose
that would have come in time as you began to
show, but for Alexander to see that already
proves his true calling is an artist. He has
vision and talent. If he can paint everyone like
he does you, my love, he could be the richest
man in the kingdom." Markus's voice cracked
as he spoke indicating what emotions had
taken him over when looking at Katrina. The
queen agreed and told Markus if he decided to
sell his paintings, she wanted one for her

bedroom. Whatever he painted would be fine, she just wanted one. They probably wouldn't be able to tell Alexander that she had one, but she didn't care. She loved him too. He was, in many ways, her son too. With his mother gone, she had filled that void for him many many times over the years. She knew deep down, he really loved her, his heart had just become so bitter, he lashed out and couldn't help himself. She hoped that Markus and Katrina could help him recover from all that. She prayed one day his heart would heal and he'd be happy again.

Markus decided he would need to start a ledger for Alexander's expenses and income from his art sales. He would then know how much money was owed to him or whatever cause he wanted to support with it. Alexander needed to see how much his talent was worth. He also knew he was going to deposit the first money with the solicitor for the shoulder and head portrait he had done. Markus would put that on his desk, but the full length was certainly meant as a gift for Katrina so she could decide where she wanted it. He was pretty sure she would be carrying it around from room to room for a while. She was truly captivated by it and had an immediate feeling of being a mother.

He was right, in the days to come he would find her sitting looking at it, touching her stomach and singing to her little Princess Anne

Marie. They were already forming a bond, thanks to Alexander.

It seemed they may owe him a little now too. He was becoming a member of their family again and he was honestly helping Markus and Katrina to expand their love for each other, the kingdom, and him as well. Markus had never seen this side of Alexander before. They were boys and young rowdy men who didn't take anything serious before; now they both knew the worth of a good woman, the warmth of a kind smile, the joy of family and the joy of belonging. He truly couldn't decide who helped who achieve all this more, but he knew they were all the better for it, and that was a very good thing.

He couldn't wait for paintings to start selling and be able to show Alexander what an impact he had on people and what a great asset he was for the kingdom. He brought people together through his paintings and that was an amazing thing that few people could do. He needed to see his self-worth, even from prison.

Chapter 8 – The Wait was Quick

The months seemed to slip by like water in the stream. Markus and Katrina spent as much time as they could spend in each other's arms, they still went for walks in the gardens and for the first three months they still rode the horses, or maybe a better phrase would be they walked the horses, but they still enjoyed being out in the sunshine and being together. They continued their bubble baths and tried to keep Katrina relaxed and happy. They watched her belly grow and measured it. Markus liked to measure it by putting his arms around her at the biggest part. They watched the seasons change and time pass. They knew their long awaited arrival would come sooner than they expected and their whole life would change. It would be some better and some worse as a baby requires a lot of attention, but mostly for the best as they would be able to hold their love in their arms and feel it like never before. Any change in a family requires work. And most of the time it's just a change in how and when things are done. Just like changing how she rode the horse, some things would be just like always and some would be interrupted by a crying baby. Yet on the other hand, she might forgo a party to play with her sweet little girl. There's as much good if not more than bad changes. It's like the rest of life, it is what you make it.

Markus made sure to pick her flowers all summer and keep them by her bedside. He wanted the baby to recognize scents. He would lay his head on her chest and his hand on her belly and talk to his daughter. He wanted her to know his voice. He personally made sure the nursery was ready for her and he bought a new rocking chair and a nice soft oversized chair with ottoman so Katrina would be comfortable while she nursed the baby. He also bought a tiny crib so she could keep her near for the first month or so. She would need to hire a nanny because their schedule would get busier year after year and they had to have someone to take care of the little ones. They had just been discussing this when Lady Penelope came in and asked for a word with them both.

"I'm sorry to interrupt, but I was wondering if you had been thinking about what you might do for a nanny?" she began. "Well actually, we've been discussing it just now." Katrina started "Do you have a suggestion?" "I do, your grace, my aunt Lilly has recently become a widow and is about to be removed from her house. She raised four boys of her own and was nanny to three girls for the Earl of Manchester. She would make a wonderful nanny and could really use the job; especially a job that comes with a room. I was just hoping if you hadn't decided, you might give her a talk." She finished. "I think that's a fine place to start." Markus responded. "Send her a dispatch and we'll meet with her on Tuesday if that would be ok. She can, of course, spend the night here before returning after our meeting." He finished. "You are so kind your highness. I shall send her word right away." Lady Penelope curtsied as she spoke and hurried from the room. She seemed so excited for her aunt, her rulers and their new little baby. Katrina knew that if Lady Penelope recommended her, she would be a good candidate.

"Well are there any other subjects we should talk about that could be resolved so quickly?" she asked. "I know it's not totally resolved, but it's pretty close. I've come to know Lady Penelope pretty well and she doesn't give praise lightly, nor would she jeopardize her position for someone that was not trustworthy. Oh Markus, I am getting so excited to have our little princess here with us. We keep saying our princess, what if it turns out to be a prince? Will you be terribly disappointed?" she asked. "Of course not, my love, we'll just have to try right away for that precious beautiful little girl we want.

Katrina and Alexander kept up a good correspondence. At least twice a month they'd send letters back and forth. She told him all about the changes in her and the house, what she had done to prepare for the baby and he would tell her what he had painted and for whom, if it were for anyone in particular. If not, it would go to the solicitor to be sold. He had sent her a painting for the nursery. It was of a farm. He'd painted the barn bright red and had put every animal family he could think of with little babies in tow. The duck had three little ones swimming behind her in the pond. The hen had a dozen little ones pecking the ground with her, there were lambs, calves, a baby goat was on top of a haystack. They were everywhere in bright colors, with flowers all around, and four little children playing. It was beautiful. He had captured exactly what Markus had asked. There was even a picnic laid out in front of a house just peeking into the picture. Sitting in the grass together by the blanket were a man and woman that looked just like Markus and Katrina. They didn't live in a house like this, but if they lived on a farm they would have, so it was very appropriate and really sweet of him to include them in this touching little family scene. He always seemed to think about the little details he added that brought his paintings to life. Like the lady bug on the flower, or the leaves falling from the tree.

Alexander was amazed when Markus sent him a tally of what his paintings had sold for and he had decided to give half of it to the orphanage. He was an orphan and he knew how it felt not to have a family. He wanted to help those children to have food and clothes and know that someone loved them and provided these things for them; even if they could not be there in person. The captain was making regular visits with Alexander and he had gone to the orphanage several times to come back and describe certain children and the building to him. Markus had painted a few pictures specifically for those children and some for the great room, the dining hall, and the classroom at the orphanage, so all could enjoy his work. Katrina thought of him often and wondered how lonely he must be. It just seemed so cruel of them, even knowing what he had done, and worst of all, what he wanted to do!

Everyone seemed to be busy and when you're busy, time seems to fly by. It was winter before any of them realized it. Less than two more months until the baby would come. In the past month Katrina had received deliveries from all corners of the kingdom. There were baby clothes for both a boy and a girl, there were bigger outfits for both a boy and a girl, blankets, hats, booties, hand embroidered linens with Prince and Princess on them. She'd received Jewelry for the princess and even a sword for the little prince. Katrina knew what would not be for this baby would be kept and cherished for the next. She was very busy writing thank you notes to everyone. It seemed the entire kingdom was readying for the new arrival and everyone wanted to be a part of it all. Most of the things were from the poorer people, who spent their time making the things for them. They were as good as the tailor or seamstress would make because they were made with love and out of their sacrifice to do it. They would cherish the thank you cards she sent them and show it off at every event or whenever they had company. It was a real treat to have something personal just to them from any of the royal family. The aristocracy would bring gifts when they came to visit or at the ball the queen would have in his honor. It would be quite a while before the gifts stopped coming. Katrina was amazed at the love they showed her family and she, as they discussed, would definitely be an approachable ruler. She would be at events for the common folk and already had a plan in mind if her child were a girl for a very special third birthday party for her.

Katrina had just dispatched someone to bring Nanny Gertrude to the castle at her earliest convenience, just in case anything happened earlier than planned. She had not had any problems from the very beginning but she did not want to take any chances. It was two weeks before the expected date.

It was at that time Katrina received a package from the prison. She knew that writing all too well, but it was a painting, she could tell from the packaging. Before she opened it, she looked over at her full portrait he had painted and she looked exactly like it. Even the size of her stomach was the same. She was again amazed at Alexander's talent. She came back from her musings and she quickly opened the package to find a new painting of herself holding her beautiful little girl.

"Markus! Come quick, I have another portrait from Alexander." She called. He was at his desk just down the hall, so it only took him a minute to be at her side. He took the painting and fell onto the settee beside her. His knees were weak and he could no longer stand. "Katrina" he began "This is amazing. Do you really think our little princess will look like this?" he asked. "I had the same reaction, but Markus, look at me and look at that full body painting he did months ago. My belly is the exact same size as that painting. I don't have that exact same dress, but I'm even wearing that exact blue right now. Yes, I'd say our baby will look exactly like this painting. Alexander has a sense of the world. He seems to know about these things and can paint them beautifully. Here's his letter, he says when he put us together, this is how she will look. My face, your hair. Darling, I think he's right." She finished. "I sure hope so, because she's perfect Katrina. I love you both so much, my love. I pray every day our lives will always be this happy and our love will continue to grow as none other." He added.

"I can't believe we have this kind of love, when our meeting was born from tragedy. From death and almost death to a bond that will transcend death to unite us even in Heaven after we depart this world. Oh Markus, I can't imagine how some people live without love in their lives. How they must be so alone without someone to share their hopes and dreams with, their daytime and their nighttime. To feel the touch and warmth coming from another human being that cares enough to die for you. To have a love so strong that you'd rather die than be without that person." Katrina leaned over for a deep passionate kiss when she'd finished speaking these words. "I totally agree, my love." Markus replied in a rather raspy voice. "I'm afraid you have to stop kissing me that way. I cannot have you like I'd like. You've only a fortnight before the baby is born. Please don't torture me this way."

Katrina leaned over and placed her head on his shoulder. "I long for you too my darling. I need your touch, I need your warmth, I need your love, and I too am tormented at times due to the constraints of carrying this baby. It won't be long before we can be two melted into one." They both held onto each other and tried to suppress the needs of their bodies. It was a hard matter and finally Katrina said "I must move. I'm going to take a walk and get a little air." Markus stood to join her. "It is a little crisp outside, it will do us both good to cool of a little. You are a temptress for sure and I will make good on your needs after the baby comes. I love you, Katrina, with all my heart." He whispered as they headed down the hallway, arm in arm, to go for a walk.

The walk and the crisp air did do them both good. They had calmed themselves and were holding hands as they walked through the courtyard. Katrina felt just a little ornery about that moment and tickled him real good in the ribs and scurried away rather quickly. He caught her quickly of course and proceeded to tickle her back. She was laughing rather heartily when she felt a sudden stabbing pain in her belly. She doubled over and her knees buckled and she headed down, Markus grabbed her and barely kept her from landing on her face. He quickly scooped her up and headed for her room. "Anne!" he screamed as he came through the door. "Heat some water, send for the doctor and hurry up here as soon as you can. I think the baby's coming early!"

Katrina had a few more sharp pains but not as bad as the first one. By the time the doctor arrived, she was feeling fine and sitting up in bed smiling. He checked her out and said it was false labor, she may have a few more episodes of it before the real time came, but it was nothing to worry about. "Rest." He told her. "You only have two weeks or less to wait, I want you in the bed most of that time, or lying on your settee. I want someone within earshot at all times in case you need help. We certainly don't want you to fall. Your baby is very healthy and has a strong heart so you have no worries if you listen to me and do what I tell you." He finished. "I understand doctor." Katrina told him. "I will do everything you say, my baby is of the utmost importance right now."

Markus gave his assurances that she would be taken care of and would rarely leave the bed. The doctor knew Markus was fearful for the baby, so he would let her take no chances. She had a pretty easy time all the way up until now, so one little hiccup this late in the game, was nothing to worry over.

Katrina behaved and utilized her entire staff to assist in her care and the care of the baby and they were all too willing. They loved her and they wanted her and the baby to be healthy, safe, and happy.

Chapter 9 – The Baby arrives

It was a very crisp afternoon and there was even a chill in the castle, but Katrina was sweating. She had gone into labor. Nanny Gertrude was there along with the doctor, Aunt Lilly (she was hired the minute they met her and had asked her to proceed with moving in), Lady Penelope, Lady Alicia, and of course Anne; who was probably more help than any of them. Her labor was very hard from the first and because of that, it was only nine hours long. The whole castle rang with applause and laughter as the doctor announced they had a daughter and both mother and daughter were fine. Markus cried as he took the baby from Katrina's arms and kissed her head. She opened her eyes and yes, indeed, she looked exactly like Alexander had painted her. Nanny Gertrude took all the credit for the delivery and they all just smiled and congratulated her on a job well done. Katrina looked very good to have just delivered a baby and Markus was so relieved all had gone well. Now he had two beautiful ladies in his life.

Markus sent a dispatch to the queen.

My dearest mother I am so glad to be the bearer of good news. I wanted to be the one to tell you that you are finally a grandmother. Princess Anne Marie was born today. She entered this world on January 21st just past 11:30 this evening. I cannot wait for you to see

*your namesake. She and Katrina are both fine
and have been sleeping for a while now.*
             Your loving and devoted son, Markus

*Once the queen read her dispatch, she sent the
trumpeters throughout the entire kingdom
announcing the birth of her granddaughter.
She also made preparation to leave for Castle
Jamison that very morning. She knew word
would be coming and had her lady prepare the
necessary things over a week ago, so there
were only a few things to gather and a few
instructions to give and she would be on her
way. She had a need to see her granddaughter,
her namesake. She was so happy for them all
and wanted to share their joy as quickly as
possible. She had waited too long for a
grandchild. She was so fearful she'd never
have one. Since she had only been able to have
one child and no grand-children for so long, she
worried it may never happen. She had lost
much sleep worrying over that subject when
Markus was younger, then he'd decided he
wanted Katrina for his bride and she was only
fourteen, so there was another wait. Now, the
baby was here and it shared her name even.
How wonderful a gift her children had given
her. She was probably just as elated as Markus
and Katrina at this moment. She may even
declare a holiday! After all, this was an heir to
her throne and her blood coursed through this
baby too. Of course if she turns out to be half
the woman her mother is, she'll be a most*

sought after young lady in just a few years from now. Oh, the musings of an old woman. She truly must hurry and be on her way. There was a princess waiting on her Queen! Katrina awoke to Markus' face beside her. She smiled and he kissed her tenderly on the hand. "Oh I think we can do a little better than that." She said and leaned over for a proper kiss. Markus was quick to oblige and when their lips parted, he slid a beautiful pearl necklace around her neck. "You've made me even happier, my love. I thank you, and wanted to give you something to remember this day and our love that made it happen. I've also bought a matching one, Anne Marie will receive on her 10th birthday." He said with another kiss. "Once you feed our lovely daughter, I hope to be able to hold her a while so you can rest some more." He smiled. "I thought men were afraid of babies." Katrina said with a smile. "Well, I'm not most men." He politely told her. "No, you are definitely the most wonderful man alive." She told him as they handed her their baby. He watched as she fed her and saw his little girl snuggle close as she'd gotten her belly full. Now it was his turn to hold her and feel the warmth of her against him and that smell. What is it about babies that make them smell so good? He didn't know, but he sure liked it, and he liked it more because it was their baby.

The Queen arrived January 23rd to see her granddaughter and to congratulate her children. She had left as quickly as possible and had urged them to make the minimum of stops. She was not concerned about herself or her ladies, they would rest after seeing the new princess. At best it still took most of two days to get there and two days was two too many. She needed to see her granddaughter.

Katrina wasn't doing anything except caring for the baby and resting, so she looked radiant when the queen arrived. She immediately jumped up and gave the queen a hug, then took her straight to the cradle to see Anne Marie. She reached in and lifted her close to her bosom. She breathed the smell in deeply and cried. "This is the happiest moment of my life." She began "Well, since Markus was born anyway." She smiled. I have a gift for you both Katrina, please fetch that bag. Katrina went to where she had pointed and retrieved a cloth bag laying by her handbag, and took it to the queen. "I've commissioned matching tiaras for you both. Her's will be a little big now, but should fit her nicely until she's about 12. I've included Sapphires for your eyes. I'm sure she has yours and deep red garnets for her birth stone. Diamonds for royalty and these tiaras are silver to commemorate Markus being the son. I've had them make three hearts inside each other for me, Markus, and Anne Marie. I hope you like them." She finished "Oh mother!" Katrina exclaimed "They are beautiful! I love them and they're so different than any I've seen. We will need to go see Alexander and have our portraits painted wearing these beautiful pieces. I miss him anyway. We write, but it's not the same as seeing each other. You have to see the painting he's done of Anne Marie and me. He did it from his mind and it's perfect. It could not have been better or closer to looking like us, had we been there. He is so talented. Did you get the painting for your sitting room yet?" "I have. He did a portrait of the palace and it's breathtaking. I truly love it and agree he's the best painter I've ever been acquainted with." She had been touching and talking to Anne Marie as Katrina had been talking to her and finally she opened her eyes and took a look at this stranger holding her. "Oh Katrina, she does have your eyes. Oh, and that little smile is precious. She's going to be a real charmer, like her mother and I'm pretty certain, she'll be full of life and into everything, just like her father." She was saying as Markus entered the room.

"Mother! Are you talking about me, without me being here to defend myself?" He laughed. She rushed over, baby in arms, and squeezed Markus as best she could without danger of dropping the baby. "I see you've been crying." He added.

"Oh Markus, how could I not? I am the happiest woman in the world right now, and she's named after me! Fortunately, she has your and Katrina's good looks, but she has my name! Oh, I really am a doting grandmother aren't I?" she asked. "It's ok Mother, I think you're supposed to be." He finished as he urged her to a chair. "I've decided I cannot be away from you any longer and now that there's a grandchild in the picture, I know we must be together. Please promise me in a month you will come to the palace and stay there. We need to be together and Katrina wants a portrait done. I know you both miss Alexander as well and we'll have to have a few parties, luncheons and all the normal festivities involved when an heir is born. The whole kingdom will want to celebrate with us. I know you love it here, but please, for an old woman, say you'll move back to the palace." She looked pitiful, hopeful, excited and determined all at the same time. Markus and Katrina looked at each other and at the same time said "Of course we will Mother." Then laughed because they spoke as one. She would have jumped up and down had she not been holding the baby. She continued to hold her for the next hour. Anne Marie drifted in and out of sleep during that time, but then became hungry so Katrina took her for feeding and as it was getting very late, the queen decided she should retire for the evening. She cried again, kissed Katrina and the baby on the head and excused herself for bed.

"Markus, I believe your mother was afraid

we'd say no." Katrina began. "How could we?" Markus interrupted. "It's our home too and mother isn't getting any younger. Besides we can make more babies there too. We can make our primary residence in the west wing and still have some privacy that way, but also be a part of one big family all together." We'll take Penelope and Alicia, and Aunt Lilly. Everyone else will remain here and take care of Castle Jamison. They've been here long enough to handle everything. I'll come back every three months for a couple days to check on things and get reports. This was always just intended for a summer estate. It's cooler here than at the palace. We may even come together and spend a month, then go back. Life will be good, Katrina, as long as we are together." He finished. "I totally agree, my love." Katrina answered and added "You must have been thinking about this to have all the details worked out." Markus smiled and said "I miss mother too and you look so beautiful all dressed up for the parties. Makes me fall in love with you all over again."

The queen stayed a week and played with and held Anne Marie as much as she could during that time. Arrangements were being made for the six who were moving to the palace. Clothes were being packed a few choice pieces of furniture, like Katrina's chair she sat in to nurse the baby, the portraits Alexander had done would be taken, but other than that, the rest would remain. Aunt Lilly was barely getting unpacked before she had to repack to move again. She never complained, but seemed truly excited to be seeing the palace and especially actually living there. Penelope and Alicia were excited about being at court again. They loved the fancy balls, the suitors who would be starting to notice them and just the opulence of it all. They were, after all, young and impressionable. Katrina remembered all the time she spent dreaming of going to those balls and wearing the fancy gowns. It seemed like a lifetime ago. She still enjoyed those things, but being in Markus' arms was way dreamier than wearing a ball gown at a fancy party dancing with all the other men invited.

Katrina didn't care if she lived in a hovel if she were with Markus and Anne Marie. She would enjoy being with the queen and Alexander. The parties were fun, but family was most important to her.

Her uncle was there the last two weeks. She wouldn't see him as often at the palace, but he'd come a few times a year anyway. He was beaming from ear to ear and almost as excited as the queen when he met his great niece. Life was sure turning out good for Katrina, and he couldn't be happier. Katrina told him he might find himself a new wife at court. He should at least come and see what was out there. He said he was now open to it, but not exactly diligently searching for a woman. If it were right, he'd know it and it would come naturally. He wouldn't have to have bells and whistles, or some big party. It would just happen. It made Katrina very happy to know he was trying to start a life for himself again. She so wanted him to be happy and to love and be loved by a good woman again in his life. He really was still young enough to start over.

Katrina arranged a luncheon for Penelope, Alicia and Aunt Lilly's families to come and visit them before they were whisked off to the palace. It could be years before they saw them again. She knew how important family was and didn't want them to be apart without at least a new happy memory to have of each other. They were all excited to see their families and their families were very excited to be coming to the castle and not only seeing their family members, but being some of the first to see the new princess.

Katrina and Anne arranged it all from the roast duckling to the fancy layer cakes for them all to take home. Each had the initials of the guest written on top. The colors were ice blue, white, and silver. The decorations and tablecloths were covered in silver snowflakes. The flowers were white with blue ribbons in beautiful silver containers in all sorts of sizes and shapes. It was truly lovely for a winter party, and not too over the top since it was a luncheon. The conversation was lively and everyone was at ease although many had never been inside the castle. Penelope and Alicia thought it was divine. It was a good luncheon and a fun time for everyone. Markus and Katrina sat at different ends of the long table, but just looking into each other's eyes was almost as good as being able to touch hands. Katrina arranged each set of family members to have a different room in the castle for some more personal time with their families after the luncheon was over. She and Markus made a short personal appearance in each room to show everyone Princess Anne Marie. Amid many oohs and ahs, Katrina let all the ladies have a turn holding her. Anne Marie didn't seem to mind at all. She cooed and smiled at them, snuggling against some of the older ladies. She must have sensed they had years of experience with children and she would be safe and secure in their arms. There were several gifts presented to her at this time. Adorable little dresses the ladies had painstakingly sewn for her, some hand knitted sweaters and booties, a gorgeous silver frame for Anne Marie's portrait, and a few silver rattles, cups, and spoons. Katrina expressed her delight and enthusiasm for every gift and thanked them all for coming to see them off to the palace. It was important they knew how much this helped their family members as well, making it easier for them to be away at court. Everyone loved Markus, Katrina, and Anne

Marie. Katrina was beaming the entire day. She had dinners prepared and served separately for each group so they could continue their time together on the personal level she knew they needed and made sure accommodations were ready for them all to spend the night. This also gave her, Markus and Anne Marie time for a private dinner as well. They would all come together again the next morning and enjoy a sumptuous breakfast before leaving for their respective homes. She truly was a thoughtful and gracious hostess. Just another trait of a great future queen.

Before Breakfast was about to be served, Katrina made a quick trip to the kitchen to thank all the staff for their hard work and dedication to making this a wonderful time for everyone involved. She also told them they would all have three days off once she, the prince, and the rest of her party departed for the palace. They could rest, shop, go visit their families, or just do whatever they would like before returning to their regular duties. She wanted them to know how much she did appreciate their assistance in making their departure a joyous time and easier on everyone. She also got a little teary when she told them she didn't know how long it would be before her return, but she would miss them and knew they would all take good care of things in their absence. "Now to breakfast!" she said, then laughed and headed toward the dining room. Markus met her at the door and they entered together. When he'd seated her and walked to his end of the table, he motioned for all their guests to be seated. The servants entered with huge trays of food and began serving everyone. It seemed everything ever eaten for breakfast was included in that meal and when it was over, everyone was full and ready to leave for home. Everyone was hugging each other and giving their good-byes, gathering their things and loading their coaches. Although sad they were leaving their families, everyone was light-hearted due to the great time they'd had and the wonderful memory they'd created.

When the last one was gone, Markus announced their own party would be leaving in two days, so everyone would need to get their things packed and prepare for leaving. All the bigger trunks and items that could be sent ahead would go by wagon tomorrow, then the rest will accompany everyone atop the coaches or in another wagon if needed. Katrina and Markus would be traveling at a slower pace due to Anne Marie, but the rest of the party would be spending only one night on the road before reaching the palace. Everyone disbursed to work on gathering their belongings while they had time.

Katrina immediately headed to the nursery to check on and feed Anne Marie. She was making mental notes as to what else she needed to mark for shipping to the palace. There would be more clothing than anything. She wanted to personally supervise the packing of her portraits. She wanted to make sure nothing happened to them. They were too precious to her and she didn't want to leave them behind as she wasn't sure when or if they'd ever return to live at Castle Jamison. This made her sad, but the sight of Anne Marie smiling at her as she picked her up, made her very happy. She just didn't think life could get any better than this moment, but she knew it was going to be better every day that she was married to Markus; and now with Anne Marie in their lives, and hopefully more children in their future, things just couldn't be better for them.

Markus made the rounds at the castle and began to give instructions on things that needed taken care of in his absence and the arrangements to be made for tomorrow's load and then the rest with everyone following the next day. While they weren't taking everything, he and Katrina had a lot to take so they would be comfortable and the palace would feel like home. He and Katrina were both pretty tired by the time dinner rolled around. She asked for it to be brought to their chamber as they wouldn't be dressing for dinner. Penelope & Alicia could eat in the dining room or their chambers, whatever they wished. She was sure they were tired too.

"How was your afternoon dear?" Katrina asked as Markus came into the nursery. "It was good, we accomplished a lot of stuff today. I've lined out who's moving us and what we need to take. I've given them a list of furniture and I trust Anne has most of the trunks ready to send?" he questioned. "She does...she's amazing. She takes everything in stride and seems to have a plan before there's a need for one." Katrina explained. "Oh Markus, I'm so thrilled to be going back to the palace, but I'm also sad to be leaving here. I love Castle Jamison and so wish it were the primary residence of the queen. I have mixed emotions about moving, but as long as I'm with you, I know I'll be happy." She finished as he put his arm around her, gave her a kiss, and offered his reasoning and plans for them as best he could. "I understand my love, I too hate to leave, but being at the palace will be good for everyone too. Mother will not only get to see us, but she'll be a part of Anne Marie's life; as well as any other children we may have. We'll get to see Alexander more often and we do need to start taking on more of the royal duties. Mother won't be able to do it all forever. She needs us and our country needs us too. At the palace, we're very visible and the people know us and see the changes we make and the things we do." He paused and added.

"We'll have our own wing and we will be very happy there. We'll have our own private time as well as time for what's expected and what we want to do too. It will be better than you think." She smiled "I know it will be wonderful, it's just that here is where we started, so it's special for me." "Well, this is where we started for you, but that coach on a lonely road is where it started for me. I have never been able to get your eyes out of my mind and I don't ever want to either. Now let's have dinner, I'm starving." She laughed and at that instant, Anne knocked on the door with their trays. "Anne you seem to read our minds and are always here with food at the exact moment we need it." Katrina laughed as she spoke the words and Anne did too, but she added "I do my best to take care of your family and Castle Jamison too. I love my job and I love living here." "Thank you Anne, you do a magnificent job and always have. This looks tasty." Markus said as he took the covers off the plates. He leaned over for a kiss and then handed Katrina her plate. She was famished and they both finished every bite on their plates. "Now, let's go look at that beautiful baby we made." Markus said as he stood up and reached for Katrina's hand. "Or do you want me to bring her to you?" he asked. "No, I'm fine and my chair is in there. I think when she's eaten, I'd like to walk for a while outside. Do you think it's too cold?" she asked. "Not if we walk fast and don't go too far. The cold air might do us good. You especially, have been cooped up inside too many days." They crossed the hall, arm in arm and stood for just a moment looking at their beautiful baby. She was smiling and looking up at them. Markus reached in and picked her up. He always seemed to get her excited. She loved her daddy and his voice just seemed to get her moving. She was wiggling her feet and waving her free arm as he talked to her and moved her around. All of a sudden, she cried out and Katrina reached for her. "Here sweetheart, I know she's hungry. She's played with her daddy as long as she could before her belly said enough."

It was beautiful to watch Katrina feed her, so he just sat quietly to watch. Anne Marie almost immediately went to sleep when she'd finished. He put her back in her cradle and waited for Katrina to get ready for their walk. He retrieved their coats and a hat for her, helped her put it on and then donned his coat as well. When they got outside, he pulled her close and kept his arm around her as they walked. He really didn't want her to get cold. They only ventured as far as the stable where they went inside to pet the horses. She hadn't ridden in months and her horse seemed to miss her as much as Katrina missed her.

"Markus, can we take my horse to the palace. I love to ride and I'm so comfortable with her?" she asked. "Of course we can. I think it's a great idea, I'll tell Sully in the morning. She can be led behind the wagon. I love to ride with you and we're already taking my horse. I just hadn't thought about yours. There's been so much to do to get ready to go and in such a short time. Is there anything else you've thought about, we might have missed? I want you to have whatever you want to be comfortable and feel at home in the palace." He finished. "I think that's all, and I hadn't thought of her till we came out tonight." I think once we get settled in, I'll be feeling strong enough for a short ride at the palace. I know life will be different there, but it doesn't mean we'll be different. I love you Markus and I love Anne Marie and will love all the babies to come. I'm the happiest woman in the world, and you did that for me. It's hard to even remember the tragedy that brought us together, but I'd go through it over and over again to have you as my husband." She finished. Markus drew her near and gave her a long deep kiss that left her breathless. She knew he loved her just as much and nothing could tear them apart. They were meant to be.

Chapter 10 – Joy and Suffering

Anne Marie was a perfect baby while traveling. The rocking of the coach seemed to soothe her right to sleep after each feeding. As the others had gone ahead, it was like a private get-away for their little family. They took their dinner in their room instead of in the dining hall at the inn. It was quiet and cozy. They enjoyed the evening like any normal couple would. Tomorrow would be back to more pomp and circumstance, but they loved that too. They enjoyed a sumptuous meal of stew and biscuits and leaned back on the bed to relax before getting ready for bed.

Little Anne Marie was cooing in her basket and Markus was holding Katrina in his arms, whispering many loving things in her ear. She wrapped her arms around his and smiled at everything he had to say. He'd told her how much he loved her, how beautiful she was, how lucky he was, how this moment was perfect. Just the three of them a world away from anyone else and any other responsibilities. Time seemed to stand still for a few minutes, then Markus turned Katrina towards him for a long and lusty kiss. She could barely breathe when he let her go. "It's a good thing I'm in bed, my knees are weak after that." She smiled looking into his eyes as she spoke. "Well then, let's be sure to take advantage of the situation, since I already have you in the bed, I think I'll have my way with you woman." He laughed as he pulled her closer and kissed her again. It could not be more intense. They loved each other mind, body and soul. This is as good as it gets between a woman and a man. The heat was rising between them and they both longed to be joined as one. They began a slow exploring of each other which quickly progressed to a very heated session of love making. Anne Marie didn't seem to notice. She slept soundly in her bed as though whatever the sounds may be from her parents were comforting, just knowing they were inches away from her. When their passion was sated, Katrina was sure they may have just created Anne Marie's brother or sister. She was in heaven and Markus had taken her there once again. He got up, dressed and picked up their dishes. "Where are you going? She asked. I'm going to get us a drink and some bread and cheese, I'm famished!" he smiled. "Get a lot!" she told him. "I'm still weak in the knees."

Markus returned in about 15 minutes with their snack. Just as they finished eating, Anne Marie woke up. Katrina changed and fed her and they were all off to dreamland.

It was strange not having a servant or two around, if people didn't take a good hard look at them, they wouldn't even recognize Markus as the prince. It was nice having a normal outing. Katrina gathered their stuff, fed and changed Anne Marie while Markus took everything out to the carriage and the three of them went in to the dining hall for breakfast. They ate a very sumptuous breakfast and just as they were finishing, the driver approached to see if they were ready. Markus nodded and he left to bring the coach around while Markus paid the inn keeper. Anne Marie was awake and cooing, but as soon as they started and the coach began to rock, Katrina knew she'd be fast asleep.

When they arrived at the palace, everything was all set up for them. Their clothes were put away and their rooms were arranged with the pieces they'd brought. The queen was waiting in her sitting room to welcome them once they'd freshened up. She hugged Markus and Katrina, then reached for Anne Marie. "My beautiful grandbaby." She said as she looked at her. "I've waited a long time for you and am so excited to have you here with your Grand-mama." She then looked at Markus and Katrina as they sat cuddled on the settee. "Did you have a good journey?" she asked. "It was very pleasant Mother." Markus replied. "You two are the most amazing and beautiful couple." She smiled. "And now you're parents. I remember when you were born Markus. Your father and I were so very happy, so I know how you feel. I also know you two are going to be great parents, and great rulers one day as well." she finished. "Mother, we're going to go see Alexander tomorrow and introduce him to Anne Marie. He's been looking forward to our return. I think we'll take Lady Penelope to help with Anne Marie, and a very nice luncheon. We'll make the most of a day of it. I'll have them ready more pillows and a basket so the ladies will be more comfortable, and Anne Marie can sleep. He's really changing mother. I know he still harbors ill will to you, but do you want to send him well-wishes? He asked. "Every step we take brings him closer to regaining a relationship with us and will help him lose his bitterness as well." He added.

"Tell him I love him and wish him well and I so enjoy his paintings. Tell him I'd like to come visit, maybe play a game of chess with him, when he's ready. We used to play occasionally when he was young. Tell him I sent him lemon cookies, they're his favorite." She finished her sentence and turned to ring for her maid. When she appeared the queen instructed her "Tell cook to prepare some lemon cookies for Alexander and a sumptuous luncheon to be taken for Alexander, Markus, Katrina, and Penelope. They're going to visit tomorrow. Also send a notice to the prison that they don't need to prepare his meal tomorrow. Oh, and I'm sure a bottle of fine wine will be appreciated as well." She finished and winked at Markus. "Mother, you always know exactly what's needed and when." He laughed.

"Katrina, you're terribly quiet today, are you well? She asked. "I'm fine, mother, I'm just enjoying lying in my husband's arms. It's been a hectic few days and we haven't had a lot of alone time. In many ways that's a wonderful thing, as Anne Marie is such a joy and with getting ready to come here, but it just hasn't given us a lot of time for me to feel those strong arms around me." She finished and Markus squeezed her tight and kissed the top of her head. "Things will get back to normal soon, my love." He told her. "I know, Markus, it's just going to be a new normal." She said. It was nearly time for dinner, so Katrina took Anne Marie and changed and fed her, freshened up for dinner and joined Markus in the hallway as he was coming to get her. Aunt Lilly was watching Anne Marie so they enjoyed their dinner and headed to bed. They were both tired and they had a big day tomorrow; but Katrina had a lot of trouble going to sleep, as she was so excited to show Anne Marie to Alexander.

The guards were bringing in extra chairs and adding pillows to them for everyone to be comfortable. They brought a table with tablecloth so Alexander knew Katrina and Markus were back; but there was an extra chair. He wondered who would fill it and finally decided it must be a nanny for Anne Marie. He was so excited to be able to hold his new little cousin. It would be good to see

Markus and Katrina as well. Their letters were great and they kept him informed about their lives, but to be face to face was what he longed for. He had only two visitors, the captain and the solicitor who came to pick up paintings and he was all business, very little chit chat, so he was in bad need of personal contact. Once a month the orphanage would bring one child for a half hour visit. The child would bring a thank you card to him for all the money he was donating to make their lives better and he would then let that child paint a picture. He would guide and help them make it look good. He hoped to inspire them to be creative and make something better of their lives, even if it was only for their own enjoyment. Those visits were good, but often strained. They were, after all, in a prison. This visit was family; and Katrina and Markus truly loved him. He'd painted a lovely picture, for Anne Marie, of a forest glen and pond with all sorts of animals, fairies and children playing. She was in the center of them all, lips pursed, blowing gently on a dandelion seed pod. The seeds were just beginning to take flight. It was adorable and he knew Markus and Katrina would love it and so would Anne Marie one day. He would ask them to hang it low on her wall so when she started crawling and walking, it would be at her level of sight and they could tell her stories about all the animals in the painting and how the children would play games.

He turned his thoughts back to the nanny and wondered what she would be like; would she be ashamed to have lunch in a prison cell, or would she just treat him and his circumstances as normal, like Katrina and Markus do? Would she be young or old? Would she be someone he'd enjoy painting? He was really getting excited to see them all. He'd bathed and dressed early. He'd straightened up his cell and made room for his guests before the guards started bringing in the extra furniture. He was also looking forward to the special meal they always brought with them. He ate well every day, but there would be special stuff, like pastries and sauces for the meat. Luxuries he didn't get as a rule. If he was lucky, even a bottle of wine would appear. Yes, this was going to be a good day. He must have checked his timepiece every fifteen minutes and finally it was almost noon and sure enough he heard them coming up the stairs.

Katrina was first, then Markus, carrying a basket full of baby. After a quick hug for each, Katrina reached in the basket and handed Anne Marie to Alexander, with proper introductions, of course. Lady Penelope was busy putting the food out and readying their lunch. She noted the cell was closed when they arrived, but the door had not been closed when the guard left after carrying in the last box. When she finished, she actually looked their way and gasped in amazement when she saw

Alexander and Markus looked identical. When she recovered, she got Katrina's attention with an "ahem" "Oh my" Katrina exclaimed. "I neglected to introduce you. Alexander, I'd like you to meet Lady Penelope of Manchester. Lady Penelope, Alexander." She cheerfully smiled at them both. Lady Penelope is my Lady in Waiting and she's assisting me today with lunch and Anne Marie.

"Hello Lady Penelope." Alexander bowed as he spoke. "I'm truly sorry I didn't visit Manchester more often, they have the most beautiful women in our entire kingdom." He added as he kissed her hand. She blushed slightly, curtseyed, and said "Hello and thanks for your kind words. Lunch is served My Lady." She told Katrina. They all sat down to a scrumptious meal and lively conversation. Alexander made sure to engage Lady Penelope in conversation. They seemed to really hit it off. They liked a lot of the same things and were as comfortable as old friends. It was all Alexander expected it to be. When they got to dessert, it was a chocolate strawberry torte.

It was then Markus gave him the lemon cookies and the queen's words of love and remembrance of old times. He was touched that she remembered. He carefully put the box of cookies on his only shelf to enjoy for days to come, and asked Markus to thank her for him. He looked a little pensive and maybe a tear was in his eye, as he took care with his special gift from the queen. He seemed to remember good times spent with her as well.

Lady Penelope set about clearing the table and putting things back in the boxes and baskets. The guards carried them down as she finished each one. She gave them the torte for their help and asked them to put the empty server in one of the baskets. She kept the wine and glasses out for Markus and Alexander to enjoy and some lemonade for herself and Katrina. The others had been talking during that time, but Alexander kept looking her way and Katrina noted that later she'd tell her how nice it was to give the torte to the guards.

Katrina moved over to lay Anne Marie in the basket and Lady Penelope whispered "I thought the guards might be a little kinder to Alexander if they didn't resent all the attention this prisoner received." "That was very good thinking." Katrina told her. "Now come sit with us and enjoy the conversation." She added.

As she moved the three feet to join them, Alexander smiled and asked if he could paint her sometime. "Of course, if it's alright with His Highness." She replied rather excitedly. "Well, you'd have to bring Katrina as your chaperone, if she's willing." He told her. "I'd be happy to do it." Katrina quickly spoke. "I may get a new sketch of Anne Marie too." She added. "It's a date then." Alexander laughed. "I'll be here whenever your calendar permits. Mine is totally open except for the first Tuesday in each month when the child from the orphanage comes." He finished. They all laughed and then started asking questions about the children. Alexander was so enthused about the one little boy, he could hardly contain himself. It was a real joy teaching and seeing the progress he was making. Anne Marie started to cry and Alexander quickly picked her up and said "If you don't stop that crying, I'll send you home." His voice was so soothing to her, Alexander sounded just like her daddy and she quickly stopped crying and went right back to sleep. "There." He whispered. "I have the touch." They all laughed again and Katrina said I hate to leave, but Anne Marie is probably getting hungry. I imagine that's why she woke up." They all stood and gave hugs and Alexander planted a gentle kiss on Anne Marie's little head.

Alexander again bowed low to Lady Penelope and kissed her hand again. "It has been a real pleasure to meet you and I look forward to our painting session." He said. All she could manage was "Likewise." A slight blush and a curtsey. He shook Markus' hand last and bade them all farewell. When they got in the coach, Katrina looked at Lady Penelope and said "I think Alexander is quite smitten with you." "Oh My Lady, I think he was just being most polite." She responded. "We'll see." Katrina replied with a smile on her face.

Katrina waited four days and told Lady Penelope they could go for her portrait session the next day if she wished and that Lady Alicia could help her do her hair. She was elated. She asked the cook to prepare a luncheon for them and decided to take some needlepoint to work on while they painted. She wanted to give them as much alone time as she could considering the circumstances. She was as excited as Penelope. She was just sure this was a perfect match. They both seemed so smitten from the moment they laid eyes on each other. It normally only took Alexander a few minutes to look at someone and he could then paint them in any position in any setting, but Katrina was sure he would need several sessions before Penelope's portrait would be completed. She didn't mind, she'd play with Anne Marie and work on her tapestry. She'd even take a blanket to cover herself should Anne Marie need to eat while they were there. She was just sure this would be the thing to totally bring Alexander out of the last shreds of his past darkness. Everyone wants to love someone and to be loved in return.

They did have three sessions, about four days apart each, before her portrait was completed.

It was exquisite. He'd painted her in a garden with flowers blooming everywhere and even one planted in her hair. Penelope was a very pretty woman, but once again Alexander brought out all her best features and more.

This non-courtship continued for several months always being touted as a portrait session, but Katrina knew better. They spent much time talking about their lives, hopes and dreams. They had a lot in common. Penelope played the harp, so she took a small one there to play for him. Katrina was very surprised and insisted she play at the next dinner they had at the palace. She was exceptionally good and Anne Marie would sit so quietly and watch her movements and listen to the beautiful sounds.

When Katrina began to show, they had to announce she was with child again. Unfortunately this baby was not to be. She lifted Anne Marie from her crib one morning and collapsed. Fortunately she cradled Anne Marie against her as she fell so she wasn't harmed, but Katrina was bleeding excessively and lost the baby. She was very distraught and had a hard time dealing with this loss. She cried for three days. Nothing Markus said or did helped her. All her old emotions came back with the new. Her mother, brother, father and now her baby were all gone. She knew she was loved, but why must she continually endure

suffering the loss of loved ones. She had not
even touched this baby and had only felt it
moving for a short time; but it was a part of
her and of Markus and now it was gone, never
to be loved, never to be held, never to know the
joy of having such a wonderful big sister. She
just didn't understand why it was always her
losing those she loved. Everyone came to her
aid to comfort and cheer her. The doctor
assured her this was not uncommon and
nothing she had done had caused it. Sometimes
God just knew best and he took the baby back
before something more horrible happened to it.
He also tried to tell her it wasn't even big
enough to consider a baby and mixed with all
the blood and after-birth that she lost with it; it
would be hard to find it in all that. It hadn't
really started its life, but Katrina knew better.
She knew in her heart this was a baby from the
moment it began to form. She knew it was
alive for she'd felt it move. She knew it had
touched their lives and brought them much
happiness. She knew it had also brought much
sorrow when it died. No, the doctor was
wrong about this. That baby was huge, it was
not mixed in, it was covered in a burial
blanket from the womb. That baby was full of
life and had increased the love between her
and Markus. That baby was important and
should not be discarded as anything else. She
needed validation for it and wasn't sure how to
get it. Markus was at her side for three weeks
before she threw him out of her room. "I love

you dearly, but I have to have a couple days alone to deal with my loss, our loss." She pleaded. "I have to find a way to make our baby's short life meaningful to everyone, as meaningful as it is to me."

"You know I had a year to grieve when my father died and it really took me that long. I don't think it will take me that long now because I am not alone. I have you, mother, Anne Marie, Penelope and Alexander, as well as the marvelous staff here that really do care about us all. I just need to be alone so I can figure out how to go on without this part of me that's no longer here. There's a pain Markus that's different than before. This life was in me and that changes things. I know I didn't do anything wrong, that sometimes those things just happen, but I still need some quiet alone time for me. I also know you are hurt and disappointed in this loss, but it's different for me. I do want to try to have more babies, I'm not afraid of that, I just have another scar inside that needs to heal. Please darling, give me two days and then we'll get things back to normal." She asked as she stared into his eyes.

He knew she was hurting and just wanted to hold her and take the pain away, but that wasn't how she needed it to be. He pulled her close and whispered in her ear. "I love you beyond measure and I understand your need and will do as you say. My bed will be outside our door. When you need me, call my name or come get me and I will be there for you. I respect your feelings and understand your needs are different than mine and I can't always bear your burdens. I just don't want to lose you too. All I ask is that you come back to me as strong and confident as before. I love you." He let her go and walked away. Outside the door he placed a chair and ordered a cot be readied for his sleep that night. She was only to be disturbed when Anne Marie needed feeding. He ate, slept and waited right there.

It didn't take Katrina a full two days to sort out her feelings and get her emotions under control, she came to the realization of what she had to do for her baby, for herself. She knew what to do, but needed help with making it come to life. She knew Markus loved her and would do anything he could do to help her, but for this event, she needed to see Alexander. So after a day and a half, she bathed, got dressed, and ordered a coach and refreshments be readied for her visit to the prison. When she stepped outside her room, she embraced Markus and told him she needed a portrait and was going to see Alexander, but she was going alone. He nodded and walked with his arm around her to the door. As she was about to step into the coach, he kissed her on the cheek and told her he would be there when she returned. She told him she loved him and would be back in time for dinner, please let the cook know she would need a place setting.

Katrina fell into Alexander's arms and cried again. She finally composed herself and asked him if he could do a portrait for her of her lost baby. She just needed a face to go with her pain. She was sure it would help her heart heal. "Of course I can." He told her. "Do you want it before you leave? The paint will be wet, but if you're careful, you can take it with you." He explained. "Oh could you really do it that quickly? It would mean the world to me." You sit there and I'll start it now. I think this one must have been a girl too, do you want it painted that way, or just a baby in a white blanket with nothing to indicate a boy or a girl?" he asked. "I think the face peeking out from a white blanket will be sufficient. You see I can't even give it a name because I don't know for sure." She explained. "I think you know deep down Katrina, but I think you should pick both names and name your baby. I think that will help you heal." He hadn't stopped painting the entire time he spoke and had the painting a little more than one third finished at that point. "If you'd like, when you decide, I can put its name at the bottom for you." He sort of asked. Katrina finally spoke. "I think we shall call this baby Joan Thomas and we shall remember it always by that name. Please do put it at the bottom of the painting so all will know from henceforth that this baby was just as important and loved just as much as one held in our arms as it was given a proper name and was an important part of this family." "Oh Katrina, you have done it again. That's a beautiful name and we have ancestors with those names, so it is a family name too." He smiled. It was only about two more minutes before he moved aside and turned the canvas for her to see. She was seated in a big cushioned chair holding a little baby in her arms. They were looking at each other and had eyes full of love. Katrina cried again, but this time it was tears of joy. "Oh Alexander, I believe you have already healed my heart. I really just needed to see my baby for that hole to be filled and you've given that to me. I will forever be grateful to you." She kissed him on the cheek and turned to go. "Be careful of the wet paint." He cautioned. "Oh, I'll not smudge this painting, it's of my baby." She smiled and left for home.

When she arrived, Markus met her at the coach. She cautioned him to be careful of the wet paint, but turned the canvas for him to look at their beautiful baby. "This, my love, is Joan Thomas, our little baby who's gone to Heaven. Didn't Alexander do a wonderful job of painting it for me?" she asked. "He did indeed." Markus replied, wiping tears from his eyes. "This was the best idea ever, now when we think of our baby Joan Thomas, we can look at this painting and be comforted by the love in its eyes." Remind me to do something wonderful for Alexander." He said. "He won't want anything." She told him. "It's his family too." She looked up, at Markus and then stretched to kiss his lips and wipe his tears. "We're going to be ok now." She said and took his hand to go inside and show the queen her second grandchild's likeness before hanging it on their bedroom wall. The queen couldn't believe it. Alexander's talents went far beyond painting. They extended to the souls of the people he met and painted. Even when he painted a flower, it seemed to be still living and ready to be picked for a bouquet. He'd never seen this baby, but he "knew" what it looked like and how to paint emotions coming from it. They were so blessed by his abilities.

Katrina and Markus went together to hang the painting in their room after the queen had seen it. They chose a very prominent place for it, right beside Anne Marie's painting and then they went in to get Anne Marie. Katrina fed her and as it was almost time for dinner, she told Markus that she wanted to take Anne Marie down as well. She would be asleep soon and she wanted to be with her for a while. He thought that was wonderful and so did the queen. This baby was a nice distraction from the one they'd lost and many more would hopefully come to fill the void, but Joan Thomas would always be an important part of their family because it was flesh of flesh and bone of bone.

Chapter 11 - Life Continues

It was good to grieve and good to know you
had done your best, even when it didn't seem
like enough. Knowing you'd given your all
was enough to let yourself be free of any guilt.
It was a good way to live your life. It was still
hard losing someone you loved. The queen had
sent criers out to announce that Prince
Nicholas & Princess Katrina had suffered the
loss of their baby Joan Thomas. It wasn't for
them to send notes, or offer condolences, it was
for them to know and remember an important
part of their family had come and gone in a
very short time and that they were grieving,
but would be back to normal functions as soon
as they could.

Anne Marie was six months old, it was
summertime and a great time to be out and
about. The fair was coming up and the people
would be able to come see the royals. Anne
Marie was just starting to toddle around some,
so her squeals of delight at everything would
amuse everyone in the kingdom. She was the
most delightful little thing and so happy all the
time. Sometimes Markus and Katrina would
nearly fight over who got to
feed her that evening. She was starting to eat
soft foods and she was loving nearly
everything she tasted.

Katrina knew there would be some to extend

their regrets of Joan Thomas, but that was going to be a good thing in her mind. She wanted people to remember she had another beautiful child that was so important to their family. They'd had a rough few months and many teary moments, but those were nearly a thing of the past. They had started planning new customs for their private times and special things they always did for Anne Marie. Every night it was a story, a kiss on the cheek and a "see you in the morning" as they put her to bed. Children needed consistency in their lives and royal children didn't ever seem to have enough of it with all the duties expected of them and the necessary duties of their parents.

The kingdom was still very stable and at peace with everyone, so most functions were simply enjoyable. Nothing stiff or tedious to attend to.

Lady Penelope and Alexander were still courting as best they could in prison. He was still painting, but a lot more of the portraits were of Penelope. They were thrilled to see him so happy. The only drawback was they knew he would never propose marriage as long as he was in prison, or hold her back from marrying someone else should another suitor arrive on the scene. Penelope truly loved the queen and she would tell Alexander stories of their time together and how wonderful she was and how kind she was to everyone. She was, unknowingly, changing his opinion of her and that was definitely a good thing.

They'd had a wonderful time at the fair, Anne Marie loved the baby animals she could pet and cuddle up with. She liked riding in the swings with her mommy and bouncing on horseback with her daddy. She also got to meet some other babies her age and played in the dirt for the first time. She was walking pretty steady, but when that baby goat nudged her, she went straight down on her bottom. She puckered up and let one tear fall before the goat rubbed up against her and licked her ear. She then giggled and pulled herself up by holding onto the goat's neck. She was sure fun to watch and everyone in the kingdom wanted to watch everything she did. It was fun for everyone and they all felt right at home on the palace grounds. They talked to the queen, who was a little more reserved than Markus and Katrina. She sat on a couch while Markus and Katrina got right in there for everything going on, including the horse race and the lawn bowling. It seemed like they'd forgotten all their appointments, the formal clothing, and even their station in life. They just plain ole had fun with all the people there.

The best part of the day was the dance at the end. Katrina and Markus danced the first dance together and then took turns dancing with everyone else at the fair. It was right then that Katrina decided she was going to have a father daughter dance for Anne Marie next summer. She would be one and a half and would love to be dancing at that age. Katrina would get started on invitations very soon and start saving dresses for any girls smaller than Anne Marie might be and ask other royals to do the same, so every little girl in the kingdom could come with her daddy and dance at the party. They would have their very own ball, just for wee ones. No fancy dresses would be allowed, so no poor child would feel embarrassed. She was mentally clicking away items as she danced. By the end of the night, she had the whole thing organized in her head.

Katrina could not wait to tell Markus, but she kept her mind mostly on her task of dancing. She surely didn't want to step on anyone's toes. She was having a great time and it was good to laugh again after so much sorrow. She would always remember what her little Joan Thomas would miss out on in life, but could only imagine how happy she must be in Heaven. God had a different plan for her and Katrina was learning to accept that plan, even though it would still sting for many years to come.

When the evening's festivities were over, she and Markus stood by the gate and thanked everyone for coming, and bid them good night. She'd long ago given Anne Marie to Aunt Lilly so she could go to bed; poor little thing was just about limp. She was so tired, but also had a wonderfully fun day.

When the last guest had gone, Markus put his arm around Katrina and led her back towards the palace. Just inside the door, he leaned over and kissed her, oh so delicately on the lips. "I've had a wonderful day, my love; but I'm exhausted. What do you think about heading to bed?" he asked. "I think that's the best idea you've had all day. If I had to do one more thing tonight, I'd probably fall over. It was a great fair though, don't you think?" she asked. "Best one I've ever been too." He grinned as he spoke. "I know, last year I spent it in the company of Alexander, pretending to be you." It was fun then too, but so much better this year with my husband safe and sound in my arms and out of harm's way." She leaned in for another kiss when she finished. "I wish he could have come this year. It was all his idea and it's such a shame he couldn't be included." "I know, my love; hopefully time will work it all out. Now, let me help you with that gown." They'd reached their room and he was not going to get Lady Penelope to assist her as he was most capable of doing so. "What do you think about a bubble bath in the morning? I'll help with all your toiletries too. It's been a while since we got to do that together." "You know I always love it when you help me and well, the baths are amazing too." She winked, giggled and crawled into bed. "Hey! Not without me you don't." he teased as he climbed in with her, pulled her against his chest and breathed into her hair. "Good night my love."

Chapter 12 –Creating Self-Sufficiency

Markus awoke before her and called for the bath to be made ready. When it was just perfect, he gently started kissing her face and head, coaxing her awake. Each kiss getting a little longer and heavier on her lips until she smiled and kissed him right back. Long and deep, showing just how much they loved each other. "Oh Markus, I do love being awakened this way, but I'm afraid if we linger too long, we'll miss breakfast with your mother and she has some things to talk to us about. I also have a couple things I'd like for us to consider." She finished. "You sure know how to spoil a moment." He pouted. "Now there, don't you pout." She pleaded. I need your attention all day and all night. "Well, now there's a proposition I'll give some thought to." He smiled and winked at her as he pulled her to her feet and into the bath. After much playing in the bubbles, they proceeded to actually get washed and dressed. It was then that Katrina mentioned the Wee Ball she wanted to have next summer. "Markus it will be wonderful for all the fathers and their little girls to have their own dance. We'll make sure every girl in the kingdom has a dress to wear, nothing fancy, just a dress, so they will all fit in and enjoy the early evening. We won't keep them out too late. What do you think?" she asked. "First of all, I like it, and it sounds like you have all the details worked out. We just need to speak to Mother about it, put the date on her calendar and send out notices so everyone will have time to plan and prepare. And ask for help, of course, should they need a dress or two." He stated. "That's one of the things I want to talk about, but I have another." Katrina began "You are sure full of yourself, what is this other spectacular idea you have my love? He interrupted. "I do think it's spectacular and just for that I'm going to make you wait till breakfast to hear it with Mother." She crossed her arms, nodded her head and gave him a firm Humph! He laughed and said "Well, I guess you told me. Now let's get down to breakfast, I'm starving after all yesterday's festivities."

The queen was just descending the stairs when they caught up with her. "Good morning children." She addressed them. "It's good to see you didn't have to sleep in Mother, from all the partying yesterday. I was afraid you'd be too tired for breakfast." Markus smiled as he took her arm. With his other arm firmly around Katrina, they maneuvered the staircase only missing their beautiful little Anne Marie in their grand descent. "There's a little life left in the old woman." She retorted, just as playfully as he'd made his comment. "Well I, for one, am full of life and energy this morning." Katrina beamed as she spoke. "She's plotting Mother." Markus explained with a smile. "But, we'll be seated in a moment and get to hear all about it. She's making me wait to hear with you. I said it must be a big one as excited as she is and that's why I'm being punished." He explained. The queen laughed and took her seat. They were immediately served breakfast and after everyone had taken a couple bites, Katrina could hold it no longer. "I have to tell you my idea." She began. "Darling, your food will be cold, can't you wait until we finish eating?" the queen asked. "I suppose it will keep a few more minutes." Katrina answered with a saddened look on her face. "Oh, alright, go ahead my dear. You look like you're going to cry if I don't let you tell us now and I never did like to let a baby cry." The queen answered.

"I actually have three ideas and a few particulars will have to be worked out and I'll leave percentages and such to Markus as that's his territory. My first idea and I've explained that one to Markus, is a Wee Ball for the girls and their fathers. It will need to be next summer so Anne Marie will be old enough to enjoy it. It may also turn into a yearly event for them and I hope it will. We just need to send invitations soon with a date, so everyone can pass dresses along to children who may not have any. Nothing fancy, we want everyone to be on equal footing, it's for fun, not for show. We'll set up a collection room for anyone having girl's dresses to donate or women's dresses for some of the older girls. If they're a daughter still living at home, they should be *most welcome to the Wee Ball. With a room full of dresses here, we wouldn't have any girl with an excuse not to come with their father to the palace for a ball in their honor. We can do refreshments for everyone. Punch and sandwiches maybe. It will be a fun time. I know I always wanted to come to the palace and dreamed of the day I could attend a ball here. I would have had that opportunity due to bloodlines, but many little girls can only dream of it. I want to make dreams come true in our fairytale kingdom. I want every little girl, for just a night, to feel like a princess, like she's the most special person on earth."*

"I want to get the whole city involved in making a garden for the orphanage. I'd like flowers and trees in the front and a real working vegetable garden in the back." I'd like to get volunteers to work with the older children to lay it out and ready the ground and do the planting. I think they could learn some valuable life skills and provide a lot of food for the orphanage as well. It also wouldn't hurt to have it look warm and inviting from the front so people may actually want to go there and spend time with the children, if they can't afford to adopt one. I believe Castle Jamison is beyond self-sufficient right now, so there should be funds there for the seeds, trees, and bushes. I do know the master of that castle and I'm pretty sure I can use my wiles on him to provide the materials for us. He's been

easily persuaded in the past. We'll only need help with the work." She finished. "I think it's a grand idea, but how will you get people to volunteer to do the work?" the queen asked. "That's the easy part, they get to spend time with the Prince and his Princess, side by side and maybe get to play with the Heir Apparent as well. Now how many citizens do you think would eat that up. Of course we'll brag on their skills and they'll have done a good deed and will feel well appreciated for it. I venture to say, some Lords and Ladies will be there, soiling their hands as well. I think I'll take great pride in helping stick some of those tender white hands in the dirt." "I think you're right Katrina. It should be a big success." Markus interjected.

"Then, when that project is finished, I'd like to start a trade program with the older children there. They would be taken in by shop keepers and land owners to learn a trade so they can be productive citizens. They teach the child and get their free labor for 6 months, then they would pay the child a partial but fair wage to work for them part time or full time as their schooling permits, since they would still be learning and not as accomplished as a seasoned professional. This way they could teach them to do things like they like it and they could trust them to do it correctly. I also think a small portion of the goods made would be donated to the school for their use or consumption. This way the school and the orphanage will benefit as well as our country because these children will become self-sufficient instead of being a tax burden to everyone. I also think it would give them a great sense of pride in themselves and a self-worth they may not otherwise have since many feel they're not good enough to be adopted. I also would need to count on you, Markus, to make a strong statement on behalf of the children that none be mistreated or taken advantage of. What do you all think?" she asked.

The queen spoke first this time. "Katrina, I think you have a marvelous head on your shoulders and will help rule this kingdom well one day. That is some brilliant thinking and no one can dispute any part of it as you're the first one getting your hands dirty, so to speak. I think Alexander's contributions to the orphanage are making it self-sufficient versus a tax burden already, so those monies can be used elsewhere, like one of the schools in need. We may even open a special school in a few years, if this takes off, that can teach trades that we don't have here. We may be able to make our entire country self-sufficient. If we never have to depend on another country for any of our needs, we will be truly secure within our borders and more confident in our future than ever before. Bravo Katrina!"

"I've never doubted I had a good woman on my hands, but I really didn't know the extent of your thinking and skills. Mother is right, you are a force to be reckoned with. I'm not sure where all your wonderful ideas come from, but truly you were born to lead a country. I'm just glad I'm the man at your side while you do it." He finished. "Oh, don't be silly. It's from being with you and around this palace and having the freedom to express my thoughts and desires that I have blossomed. I want to make a difference in lives and I want our kingdom to grow and progress in the best ways possible. We all have to be on board with the plans and each add our own ideas to the table to see it grow and turn into the things we want it to be." She finished.

"Katrina, I think you will need to be the one speaking to the students about your idea, or both of you. I think you can get them excited about it. Without their cooperation, it will never be a success. Markus, I'll get a dispatch ready for the Lords, when would you like to meet with them to explain your ideas so they can get everyone on their lands participating?" she asked. "How about a week from today Mother? That will give them a few days to get excited about something new going to happen. If we can keep them excited, we'll win them over." He said. Katrina spoke up and said, "I don't think we'll have a problem with their participation. I think they'll want to make an impression on the throne and many of the shopkeepers do not have children or their children have grown and they've no one left to pass their skills on to. It would be like adopting a child without having to keep them all day every day and provide all their needs. They get something in return for all their efforts. Plus it will give them more credibility and honor with the people as well. Everyone likes to patronize someone who's giving of their skills and goods to help others, especially when it's children. I think the business they'll gain will definitely contribute to their participation. We may even make those shops first priority for the palace's needs as well."

"Katrina, are you sure you're up to all these projects? It will be a lot on your plate." "I know, I need something to do, something that is productive, something that will take my mind off my woes for a short time. Watching something else grow, by our hands, will help me, I'm sure. I still have days I really miss my little Joan Thomas, but I know that it will get easier, the busier I am; and oh my what a worthy cause, helping other children have a better life. It will be exactly what I need. I thank you for asking though, because sometimes I think I could easily get in over my head before I've even realized it. I just want to be involved and do things. I want to feel life!" she almost shouted, she was so caught up in her feelings and emotions of the tasks they were beginning. And they were doing them all together, not just as a husband and wife, or rulers, or a family, but as a kingdom. It was amazing to think she had the spark that was about to ignite a country. Now that's inspiring and uplifting. Definitely good for the soul and one's spirits. Katrina was grateful to have access to the means to do it all. The hard work wouldn't matter to her. She would be enthralled and her spirit would be captured by everyone around her. "Oh Mother, I just thought of the most wonderful addition to our plan. I'd like to request that whenever we start a school and I know we'll be able to in just a few short years; could we please call it The Joan Thomas School of Tradesmanship?" she asked. "It would mean so much to me, us. I know Markus has a hole in his heart as well that Joan Thomas' passing left there." She finished. "I think that's a wonderful idea and a beautiful name! It's done! We're naming it after my second grandchild." the queen exclaimed!

Markus knew he was definitely one lucky man and his kingdom was one lucky country. He didn't think it could, but during just that breakfast, his love for her tripled. She was truly an exquisite woman and she was his. His heart soared at that moment and his face shone with the love he had for his beautiful, smart, loving, giving, courageous, thoughtful, understanding, full of life wife.

The week flew by and Katrina was just as excited as the day she'd presented her ideas to the queen. She and Markus both had written lots of notes and calculated the wages and donation amounts that the businessmen and landowners or sharecroppers would be expected to contribute. They were a little shy of where they should have been to start, but figured they needed a little extra for the teachers to entice them. They would see some pretty quick profit and would start bragging about their situations and others would quickly want to join in and be a part of it all. Katrina was also making notes of the types of trades they would need to teach at the school they'd open. She knew in her heart that it was going to happen and would feel pride and happiness that her little baby would be recognized for generations for their contribution for this country. She'd been asking questions to find out what country had the best of the best so they could bring in teachers from there for each trade. Markus kept telling her she should have been a business woman. She had so many ideas and the drive to see them through. He felt she could accomplish anything she set her mind to. She'd just smile and remind him that these skills were born from when he was kidnapped and she had to learn to think quickly and adapt to all the different situations required to keep him alive and the kingdom safe. Once again, he was the one who made her what she was.

The lords came and were very much enthused about the programs. They jotted down the date for the Wee Ball, made notes and gave their opinions for the apprenticeship program as well as who would be the best to approach first. Those with good influences for the children and those who may improve their disposition if they had a young adult around for them to mentor; especially knowing, the crown would be checking up on them. They felt it just might be a big help to those people's character as well as the benefits it would bring for the children. They saw the vision and realized it would ease future tax burdens on them as well. Nearly every one of them signed up someone to help with the garden projects at the orphanage, and those who didn't sign someone up that day declared they'd find out who wanted to and definitely send them along at the appointed date. They knew it would make the area more appealing to the eye as well as sustain a lot of the burden of feeding the inhabitants there. Everyone left the meeting with a positive attitude about everything and nearly as much excitement as Katrina to see it all through.

Katrina would oversee the garden projects and Markus was going to get started interviewing mentors for the apprenticeship program. He was starting with the students. He'd asked Katrina to join him for this part. He wanted to get to know a little about each child and what they might like to learn, or had an interest in, so he could match them up with the best mentor for a good outcome. He knew if they put a child who wanted to paint in a job of digging in the dirt, it just may not work out. Some would want to work with their hands and others with their minds. They needed to be good matches for the program to succeed and he was going to do his best to make everyone happy. As well as matching the trade they'd like to learn, he'd need to match the characters of the people they were to work with. He loved being around the children and decided this would be some good parent training for his own children when they were big enough to learn to deal with different situations and how to teach them to be diplomatic in all affairs of state.

After that meeting, Katrina wanted to go see Alexander and get his input on the layout of the flower beds. She'd already spied out an area in the back corner of the property that would do nicely for the vegetable garden. It got the morning and evening sun, but there was a huge elm tree giving shade to it during the heat of the day. This would protect the garden from the harsh sunshine that tended to wilt vines before they had a chance to grow and get strong. Oh it was all so exciting and yet still so much to be done.

Chapter 13 –Back to Prison

"Good morning, My Love." Katrina began. "Do you think we have all the balls rolling on all the projects except the flower gardens and trees in front of the orphanage?" Katrina asked. "Why yes I do and things are progressing nicely, I might add. Why? Is there a problem?" He countered. "No, I just think it's time to visit Alexander. We've been very neglectful. I know Lady Penelope has been keeping him company but we need to fill him in on what's going on and I want him to give us a layout for this project. He has such a good eye for design and how things would and should look. I think his opinion would be invaluable. Are you up for a visit and lunch there today?" she asked. "I think today is clear enough to do that. You'd best get your pretty little rump downstairs and discuss it with cook, she'll have your hide if you wait too late in the day. You know she loves to make a big presentation and extra special goodies for us to take." He finished. "You're right, I'd better get with it." She spoke as she started climbing out of bed. "Now hold on just a moment!" Markus said as he pulled her back into his arms. "I think I need to be addressed before you talk to cook. He kissed her deeply and looked into her eyes, smiled and said "I'm so glad I married you! You are a wonderful woman, Katrina" "I'm the happiest woman in the world." She answered, kissed him back and then got up to attend to the needs for the day. "I'll see you shortly at breakfast." She said over her shoulder as she went to Anne Marie's room to check on her and feed her breakfast to her.

"You've got a big day today Anne Marie. We're going to go see Cousin Alexander! Aunt Lilly, why don't you tell Lady Penelope so she can get things ready for all of us to visit today and have lunch there while I feed my precious little baby." "She's not much of a baby any more, she's growing like a weed." Aunt Lilly laughed as she said it, then turned to go find Lady Penelope. "Mama has big plans for you, my girl." She smiled and used her favorite baby voice to talk to her daughter. "May be we can tear Alexander away from his admirer long enough to talk business with us. I'm sure you won't be much help in that department, he'll want to play with you too." She laughed. Aunt Lilly was back just as she finished feeding her. "I'll take over now." She said "That worked out perfectly, I have to dress, have breakfast and get a lot of things ready to discuss with Alexander today. "Thanks Aunt Lilly. I'll be back to collect our little one at half past eleven."

Katrina hurried down the hall to dress and gather her thoughts, they hadn't seen Alexander in a while and she wanted it to be special for him today. She hurried to talk to cook before she went into the dining room for breakfast. Markus and the queen were just sitting down, as he'd glimpsed her heading toward the kitchen and knew she'd be right in. "Good morning Mother, I hope you are well this morning." Katrina began as she entered the room. Do you think you might like to accompany us to the prison?" she asked with an eyebrow arched and a smile on her face. "I trust he's not ready for my visit yet." The queen answered. "But I hope to be able to go soon. I think our Lady Penelope is filling his head with good things about me. She may just be my salvation in winning him over again." She added. "I do miss him so. I trust you are getting his artistic opinion about the flower beds?" she inquired. "Yes we are, but we really miss him too. We've been so busy, we just haven't had time to get there. I'm sure we're not missed as much as Lady Penelope would be, if she dared to miss a day going to see him. I will make it my mission to find a way for those two to marry and be happy. I just know something will change for the good for them. They are so much in love and deserve happiness. There just has to be a way." She finished as she finally started eating her breakfast. They discussed a few other ideas about particular plants and flowers the queen liked and breakfast was over. Now, they were full of anticipation about going to the prison for lunch. It still seemed strange to be so complacent about the royals lunching with a traitor to the crown.

The guards had told Alexander he would be receiving extra visitors today and a special lunch, so he knew he was finally going to see his family again. He was missing them. He was growing fonder of Lady Penelope, but he needed to see Markus and Katrina. He'd even thought of asking the queen to visit, or have him brought to her if she didn't want to come to the prison. He really wanted to apologize to her, but felt he needed to do it face to face. He'd tidied up his art supplies and made his bed. He'd even shaved fresh today although his stubble was barely showing through. He always wanted to look his best and make the best presentation possible from a prison cell. He was talking to one of the guards when he heard the commotion below and knew they'd arrived. He was like a little boy on his birthday, all jittery and about to explode with anticipation for who was about to come through those doors. He sure hoped they'd brought Anne Marie. He was missing so much of her life. Little ones seem to grow up overnight and she was already well on her way to being the one in charge. He laughed at that thought and just as he did, the door from the stairway swung open and Katrina come through carrying said munchkin he'd been thinking of. He rushed to meet her half way, squeezed them both, and took Anne Marie as he was speaking. "Come here my little pet." He said in his best and most gentle voice so as not to scare her, since it had been so long since

139

she'd seen him. "Alexander, she'll never be afraid of you, she thinks you're her daddy. You look and sound just like him." Katrina laughed. "I forget that sometimes." He answered. "I just was thinking she might be afraid in new surroundings with a new person taking her; but you're absolutely correct, she's as happy as can be." He turned to greet Markus and Lady Penelope before giving Anne Marie some more of his attention. The women started getting the lunch ready while Markus and Alexander played with Anne Marie and talked some man talk. Occasionally, Anne Marie would seem a bit confused about how daddy could be beside her and she'd turn her head and he was already on the other side of her. She was funny to watch then. She'd soon learn there were two different men who looked just alike. When they had lunch set, Markus placed Anne Marie on a blanket they'd brought and gave her a couple toys to play with. She was quite content to occupy herself just a step away from the others.

"I've missed you all so much!" Alexander began but Markus interrupted him with "Well, not all of us." And he added a wink for good measure. "Lady Penelope and I do so enjoy each other's company." Alexander added. "In different circumstances, that would be greatly different for us as well. I suppose time will decide where we go with our relationship." He smiled at her and kissed her hand. "So what brings you all to visit me?" he asked. "We have several projects going on and wanted to fill you in and ask your opinion on some of them." Markus began "But let's wait till lunch is over so we can thoroughly enjoy our food. I do believe we have venison today. Now isn't that your favorite?" He asked "It sure is!" Alexander replied and I think I smell lemon cookies too. Did the queen see to that?" he asked. "She must have." answered Katrina. "Because I didn't order them for lunch." She finished. "Tell her I said thanks and would you please take her a letter I've written asking for an audience? I really need to apologize and I'd rather do that face to face. They could take me in chains to see her if she doesn't want to come here for the visit." He added. "I'll be happy to." Markus replied. "I think she'll be very happy that you want to see her. She misses you too Alexander." "I know...and I know it's my fault we've not remained close, but I'm a different man now Markus. Please help her to see that. I know she can't do anything about my punishment, but having her forgiveness means the world to me." He finished. Lunch just seemed to be happy from that moment. Everyone was laughing and sharing amusing things from their lives, and a couple funny stories from the boys' childhoods that made them all laugh.

Finally they decided they'd better get to discussing the projects going on in the kingdom.

"I'd love to help. If you'd get me the measurements of the grounds in front of the orphanage, I'll do a portrait and even give you dimensions of every bed and what to plant in them and which trees to plant where to get the best effect for growth and pleasantness to the eye." He said with much excitement in his voice. "You certainly have a lot going on and it will all help the kingdom. It will change things for the better and will make the children there feel like they have a place and a purpose in life. It's a good thing you're doing. I'm glad you let me be a part of it." He finished. Katrina grabbed his hand, "I knew you would be able to make it beautiful. You have such an eye for how things fit, even down to making a design out of the shadows of the plants had we asked for that." She exclaimed.

"Oh and I do want to thank you for Joan Thomas' portrait. I've left that part out. When we start the school, it will be named after our baby we lost. I'm so glad everyone will know how important that child was to our family and their name will live on for generations, just like the rest of ours. It's helped me so much and I'll never be able to thank you enough." She wiped a tear as she finished speaking. "How about we call it all even." Alexander smiled. "Here, Here!" Markus exclaimed and they all laughed and forgot they were in a prison cell, they were just family enjoying themselves in each other's company. They visited and talked till four and agreed they'd have Lady Penelope deliver the required information back to Alexander tomorrow so he could tell them what they needed as quickly as possible. They needed to get started on part of it soon. Only a couple months left before planting season.

The minute they left, Alexander began to sketch. He knew the measurements would have to be taken into consideration, but he was pretty sure he'd remembered the grounds enough to make a rough sketch anyway. He loved to draw and paint. This project would give him more purpose in his work. He'd paint the finished work and donate it for the orphanage or the palace, whichever the queen and Katrina wanted. It would say "The Joan Thomas School of Tradesmanship" across the top. He liked the sound of that and knew Katrina would be ecstatic. He could not believe the ideas she had, they were brilliant and would mean so much to so many people Their country was at peace and everyone seemed happy, but this would unite the country as much as anything could. The people working together with the common good for everyone. There were no losers with these plans, but many many winners and benefactors from how it would be laid out. He was truly proud to be a citizen of this country. We'll except he'd officially been banished; but that didn't matter it would always be his home.

Chapter 14 – Hope Springs Again

Throughout March, everyone was implementing their plans and taking on their apprentices. They started slowly so they could monitor their success and soon the whole program was in full production. The beds were readied for the orphanage and trees and seeds had been ordered. It was almost time to plant everything. They'd decided, with Alexander's help to use a lot of bulb flowers so they wouldn't have to buy seeds every year. They also started a seed saving program. If it worked well, they'd have all the seeds they'd need for future projects, but could sell some as well. Maybe give packets of seeds to patrons as a small thank you. Katrina's mind was constantly thinking of things to do to improve upon their programs. Maybe even have a dinner to raise funds and use them as favors at each plate and seedlings for the centerpieces. There just seemed to be no end to it all. There had actually been three children adopted after their mentors had gotten to know them a little. Katrina and Markus had worked side by side with the Lords, Ladies, and common folk alike. No one was more important than the children during this endeavor.

Katrina and Markus almost forgot their anniversary on April 20th. They'd been working hard every day and sometimes late into the evening, planning and making arrangements, checking details and of course spending time with Anne Marie.

Fortunately, Alexander remembered and sent them a fabulous painting of the four of them. Markus, Katrina, Anne Marie, and Joan Thomas. It was amazing and Katrina cried. He'd also sent a huge cake from the town baker and two dozen roses in a beautiful vase. The note said "Nothing can compare to the love you two have shown me and the acceptance of me back into the family. I am forever in your debt. Happy Anniversary to the most beautiful family I've ever seen. All My Love Alexander" They laughed and kissed. Markus had prepared a few months back with a gorgeous sapphire necklace, so he ran upstairs and retrieved it from its hiding place and presented it to her, asking her to dress fancy and wear it to dinner. The cook had just so happened to remember as well and had several delicacies prepared for their dinner that night. The queen had invited Katrina's uncle and his consort. He had not been to the palace for nearly a year. This would be a special treat for him and Katrina. He longed to see Anne Marie and he brought a special doll for her. He also brought a silver rattle for the next baby to come. It seemed that everyone was prepared except Katrina. She felt really bad that she had nothing to give Markus. "Don't worry, my love, you give me everything I could ever want, every day." He smiled

Katrina was almost to the point of hiring someone to oversee all the programs as it was quickly becoming too much for she and Markus to handle. He agreed and there should be sufficient funds for the orphanage to pay the salary. There was just so much to do. It had become a very successful program and with their other responsibilities, they just had to have full time help. Katrina lined up a few folks for Markus to interview. They settled on a middle-aged man with enough experience in finances to do the job, but more importantly, enough energy and backbone, to get in there and work with them. He was immediately drawn to the children and enjoyed their company as much as they did his. He also seemed to take an interest in Lady Alicia as well. "Markus I fear I may lose two ladies in waiting through our projects. I may have to start all over training new girls." She confessed to him one night as they readied for bed. "I did notice a few glances in her direction, myself." He laughed. "It will be ok, my love, we're good at making changes and assisting those in love."

The Wee Ball was coming up soon too. Katrina had pulled Lady Alicia into that one as well, organizing dresses that had been donated and dispatching dresses to those in need. She'd helped Katrina finalize the food, music and obtain a final count of those attending. It was going to be huge, but Katrina had hoped all along it would be a great success.

It was now the middle of June and everything was falling into place. All the projects for the orphanage were in full swing and running themselves. Katrina just had to do consulting work and she did some of the follow up visits to make sure everyone was doing what they were supposed to be doing. Markus was in the same position. His load had diminished greatly once it all started and after they hired Lord Burtram to oversee everything. The Wee Ball was in three weeks and that was all planned as well. Katrina felt she could take a couple days off and play with Anne Marie and rest a little, she'd become quite tired these last couple weeks. Just everything catching up with her, she thought.

For two days, she did nothing but dress, play with Anne Marie, eat, rest, and sleep. She felt much better and Markus could tell. She had her old glow back. "I think you were doing too much, my love. You were looking a little tired. I'm so glad you decided to take a break." He commented on the second morning. "I think I have been too, so I'm going to take the next two days off and join you both. I am in need of some family time. We'll ride and go for walks, Anne Marie is old enough to enjoy bouncing on a horse. We'll play in her room, maybe I'll take you girls shopping. We can also eat at the fancy inn they just built in town. It will be fun." He finished. "Oh Markus, I've had a wonderful time doing all the projects and even the hard work was enjoyable, but I really have missed our time together as a family and alone, just the two of us. Maybe we can take time for a couple bubble baths and even a breakfast in bed, or two." She winked at him and smiled. "I totally agree; but I think we should have 3-4 of those. We need softened up some, our hands are getting rough. Especially yours, my love. I'll attend to those during our baths, you can instruct me again on which oils to use for what. I love taking care of you." He winked this time and they both laughed. They'd had alone time, but not a lot. They'd continued to make love regularly, but it just wasn't slow and time consuming as they'd like it to be. They were tired and had another busy day following, so they had to get busy and then get to sleep.

The two days turned into four before Markus and Katrina truly had to make some appearances. It just gave them renewed strength to keep up the good works. They were so happy at home and as contributors to their kingdom. One day they would rule, but were quite content to help things progress and get ready for the future that would one day they would be in charge of. No need to rush things, there was still a lot they needed to learn and experience they needed to gain.

Chapter 15 – The Waiting

It was just days before the Wee Ball and Katrina woke up feeling not so very good in the tummy. She was quite queasy. She rang for Aunt Lilly and asked her to help her with a cool cloth and some tea. She explained how she felt and saw a big smile come to the woman's face. "What is it? Why is this so amusing?" Katrina asked. "My child, you are going to have another baby. Did you not have the sickness in the mornings with your other two?" she asked. "No, I did not." Katrina replied. "I have been so busy, I didn't even realize that I had not experienced the monthly curse. I was pretty tired, but I thought it was due to all the programs I'd been overseeing and the physical work I'd been doing. Do you really think I am with child?" She continued. "Sure as I'm standing here!" Aunt Lilly exclaimed. "Shall I fetch Master Markus? I know you'll want to tell him. He'll be so happy. I won't let anyone else know until you make an announcement. I am so happy for you both! For all of us!" she laughed and gave Katrina a big hug, then hurried off to gather the things Katrina needed. She was back in less than a minute with a cool cloth and in less than two more minutes, she had tea for her. "I sent word to Master Markus that you needed to see him within the hour, if possible. I didn't want to alarm him. I also brought you some dry bread for you to nibble on. It will give you something in your stomach, but won't irritate it. You'll need to eat light for a few days to avoid this and I'll gather some ginger for some tea that will help you more." She explained.

Katrina was starting to feel better within just a few minutes. She was so grateful for Aunt Lilly and her expertise. It was just a few more minutes before Markus arrived. By that time she was refreshed, feeling fine and about to get dressed. He immediately looked worried when he saw she was still in bed. "What's wrong, my love? He asked. "You look beautiful and refreshed, but you're not out of bed and that's very unusual, unless my summons was more of the nature of me joining you." He grinned. "You're welcome to join me, but I want to talk right now. I have news to tell you." Markus came and sat on the bed beside her as she continued. "I really hadn't been paying attention with everything we've been involved in and all the work we've been doing, but this morning I was very sick to my stomach and Aunt Lilly suggested, and I've since thought about it and can confirm, that I am with child." Markus grabbed her and squeezed her tight. "I'm so happy!" he squealed between planting kisses on her lips, cheeks, forehead, and anywhere else he could get to. "Oh Katrina, you've given me a wonderful gift today. Do you know when we can expect our little bundle of joy?" he asked. "Well, by my calculations, it should be near the end of

February, or first of March; but Markus, I
want to wait to make the announcement. We
can tell our family and staff, but I'd rather not
make it known to the kingdom just yet. Just in
case." She pleaded. "Of course, darling; it has to
be a little scary with what happened with Joan
Thomas. I understand completely. It will be
our little secret for now; although I'm not sure
how long I can conceal my joy from those
around me. When they see my leaping from
the rooftops, they're bound to know something
is up." He joked. "I love you so much! I just
know things will be ok this time. You're
healthier than ever before and I believe our
baby will be too. Keep smiling and positive
thoughts in your pretty little head." He
finished. "Since I'm here, I'll help you with
your bath, dressing and hair. I miss that.
We've been so busy!" She told him that Aunt
Lilly thought she might have this sickness
every morning for a while, but was going to
keep her in ginger tea and stale bread to help
with it. It had sure worked this morning.
They decided to go down and tell his mother
first thing and then head to the prison to tell
Alexander. They'd tell the personal staff in a
meeting tonight and then the rest of the
kingdom in a month or so.

The queen couldn't believe it. She was as
excited as Markus. She immediately started to
ring for the butler, but Markus stopped her just
in time to explain they'd like to wait just a bit

and only tell the personal staff. She agreed and since they were all in agreement, they had tea and told cook to prepare a quick lunch for them to take to the prison.

Alexander was so excited to find out. He held her hand, looked into her eyes and told her not to be afraid, this one was going to happen. God would doubly bless her because of her former loss of Joan Thomas. "I sure hope so and thank you for always saying the right thing." She said as she hugged him. They enjoyed lunch with him and Lady Penelope, of course, before heading back to the palace. She'd dispatched a letter to her uncle and felt much better about everything. Maybe if she were the sick one, the baby would be ok. That was the thought she was going to hang on to.

Katrina did have some sickness the next three mornings, but Aunt Lilly was right there just as she woke up with bread and ginger tea. She was a God send; it only lasted about fifteen minutes before she was well again. Today was the day of the Wee Ball and she had to be well and help with final arrangements. Lady Alicia was already on top of everything. She had the ballroom being prepared, had checked on the food and musicians for the evening. Katrina had been approached by an elderly gentleman asking if his granddaughter could perform at the ball. Katrina heard her sing and immediately scheduled her for four songs. Her voice was amazing and everyone would need a break from dancing to have some refreshments. It would be a perfect time to have her sing. She was only fourteen but sang like a professional. Next year she'd schedule auditions for more performers, all children of course. Things just seemed to have a way of falling into place. She decided that was God's way of giving His blessing on the event.

She was playing with Anne Marie when Markus came in and swooped her up. He told her they were going to dance and was practicing some of the moves they would be doing. It was so much fun to watch. Katrina could hardly wait two more hours for the ball to begin. Anne Marie would laugh or giggle every time Markus swirled her around. Katrina knew in her heart right then, that the Wee Ball would be a forever thing held every year at this time. Every little girl would have her day to be a princess in a real life palace with a real life prince and princess (or someday King and Queen) as their hosts.

Katrina had put the cutest little white day dress on Anne Marie with a gold bow in her hair, reminiscent of her father's attire at their first dance. Katrina wore a sapphire blue gown to match her eyes, no frills, no fancy jewelry, she did not want to outshine any of the honorary princesses there. The evening was grand, the weather warm with an ever so soft breeze blowing, just enough to keep the dancers comfortable. The musicians were wonderful and Ariel, the young singer, was once again amazing. The food was delicious and every dance was picture perfect! Katrina wanted to dance with Markus all night long, but she knew this was not her night. Anne Marie had delighted everyone. She loved being twirled in her daddy's arms, she loved being held by him while they took breaks and talked, she loved the music and was totally mesmerized by Ariel's voice. She just watched and stared at her. She loved to clap with everyone. The only way it could have been any better for her would have been if she were a couple years older so she wasn't getting so sleepy before it was over. Katrina rang for Aunt Lilly to come get her. She took her from Markus and met Lilly in the hallway. Markus took this opportunity to dance with a few of the young ladies who were not escorted by their fathers, but by a brother, uncle or friend. It absolutely made their evening getting to dance with the prince. Every single one of them came to Katrina at one point or another and thanked her for organizing the Wee Ball. They loved it and hoped she would continue doing it every year. Although they were dressed in their simple dresses, they all fit in and felt a part of it all. They all felt like princesses and their fathers were so proud of them as well.

Unfortunately the time arrived when they

must all head home, some had to stay overnight and some had a long trip home that night, but no one minded. They had a treat they would not soon forget. They were tired from the dancing, but exhilarated from the atmosphere. Their bellies were full and their hearts were merry. Katrina and Markus stood by the door thanking each in turn for coming. When the last guest had gone, Katrina and Markus turned to the musicians and she thanked them for the beautiful music and for playing until everyone had gone. Markus put his arm around her waist, looked at the band leader and nodded. They began to play the same song they had danced to at her Masquerade when they'd first danced. Markus pulled her close and began to twirl her around the dance floor like he'd been wanting to do all evening. "The Wee Ball is over, my love; but our ball is just beginning. I've asked them to play two songs just for us. I've had a wonder-ful time dancing with my daughter, but I love dancing with my wife too. Thank you for this wonderful ball and thank you for being my wife." When he finished, all she could say was "Oh Markus, I love you with all my heart. You have given me a perfect ending to a perfect evening. Thank you!" When they'd finished their two dances, they again thanked the band and headed upstairs to bed.

Katrina again woke to that churning in her stomach and within seconds Aunt Lilly was there with bread and tea for her. "You are amazing." She managed to say between bouts of nausea. It only lasted about ten minutes and then she was good for the day. She would not be able to function without the care of this wonderful lady. She was never more thankful they'd hired her than she was right now.

Katrina's morning sickness only lasted about two weeks which wasn't much to endure at all she decided. She felt great otherwise and her baby seemed to be healthy as well. She was starting to show just a bit, since she had such a small frame it was hard to hide even a few ounces of weight gain. She'd been checked by the doctor and he agreed the baby should arrive by the first of March at the latest. Katrina had asked Aunt Lilly if she was up to assisting and probably taking charge of the delivery. Although Nanny Gertrude would be there, she really wasn't much help when Anne Marie was born, but she did take the credit for delivering a fine heir to the throne. Lilly told her she was up for the task, but thought it would mean a lot to Anne, if she sent for her to come and be the one in charge. Lilly would assist her any way she could. Katrina realized how humble Lilly was and wanted to show her thanks for the kindness Anne had shown her when she was at Castle Jamison. She decided right then that Lilly was noble as well as loving, caring, kind, and respectful of all she knew.

Katrina dispatched a letter to Anne telling her of the baby to come and asking her to plan on making the trip to the palace in January so she could be there for the delivery. Katrina told her how much she appreciated all she'd done for her during her first delivery, and how she knew things would get a little lax and maybe behind at the castle without her there, but she was much needed here.

She then spoke with Lady Penelope about what sort of gift she could get for Aunt Lilly. She wanted to show her appreciation for taking care of her during her morning sickness and for the wonderful job she was doing with Anne Marie. Penelope seemed a little cautious about recommending something for her so Katrina told her to go to the dressmakers and pick the material for two new dresses to be made for her and then go to the jewelers and pick out a locket for her, so she could keep one of her loved ones close to her heart. Katrina gave her a note to take to each business giving her authority to take care of her request. She also made a mental note to talk to Markus about something for Anne as well. Without her the castle would probably be in ruins and Katrina would have had a horrible time with Anne Marie's delivery, and now she was assisting again.

When she and Markus were in bed talking, she told him of the gifts she'd ordered and what his idea was for her to do for Anne. He loved the idea and told her she should give Anne a note when she got here so she could choose her own materials and then get her a silver dressing set, like Katrina had with a brush, comb and mirror. Anne had long hair as well, but kept it put up, so that would be useful and thoughtful as well. Anne would like that kind of gift. Katrina said they should send chocolate with the driver who went to get Anne; enough for the entire household to have some. It was a treat that most people in the kingdom would never experience and since they couldn't be there, it would be their way to say, celebrate with us, we've having a baby! Markus loved that idea too and since it would be winter, it would travel well without melting. They both missed being at the castle, but knew the palace would probably be home for the rest of their lives, or at least until they were old and gray and their son or daughter was ruler.

Katrina decided she was going to rest for an hour every afternoon, right after lunch, so she wouldn't get too tired until the baby came. Many afternoons, Markus would hold her in his arms and rest with her. He would often talk to the baby and rub the tiny bulge beginning to form there.

They decided to make the announcement the end of August so there would be six months left before the baby came and people could get used

to the idea and get ready to send their gifts.
Many would hand make items for the baby,
like before and they would need time to do
that. It was the ruler's family and they always
enjoyed being a small part of anything to do
with their personal lives. Plus everyone loved
a baby! They talked to the queen and she made
the appropriate plans and declaration to be
announced. Again, every village and town
would receive a dispatch to read the
announcement in the middle of the village or
town. The queen wanted every citizen to know
they were important to the royal family.

Katrina sent word to her favorite dressmaker
in Manchester for a couple new gowns for her,
she seemed to be growing faster with this baby
than either of the other two. She also ordered
more girl and more boy items. They had
started making preparations in the nursery
and were transitioning Anne Marie into the
adjacent room. She would have a "big girl" bed
and her own space away from the new baby.
She went with Katrina to pick out cloth for her
bedding and curtains. She really had a keen
eye for a toddler. There wasn't really much to
do, but yet it seemed like a whole lot to do.
Katrina made a list and was checking it off as
things were finished. Lady Alicia was so much
help to her. She again reminded Markus that
she would need another lady in waiting as
Lady Penelope was otherwise occupied so much
with Alexander. She wouldn't have it any

other way, but she did need some more help, now that there would be another child in the palace. He agreed and she spoke with the queen about recommendations. They scheduled a luncheon for the second week of September (just after the announcement would have been made public) and sent invitations to the Lords to present their daughters for selection.

Time seemed to fly, and it was time for the announcement to go out. Katrina was twice as big at three months with this child as she was at the same time with Anne Marie. Anyone who had seen her out and about would have figured it out by now; had they been close to her at all.

She was glowing as she, Markus and the queen stood on the balcony of the palace as the declaration was read in front by the crier. There was quite a crowd gathered and they cheered for them each in turn. They requested the prince and princess favor them with a kiss. Markus gladly obliged with a nice long one, which sent more cheers up. Then he stood behind Katrina and turned her sideways to the crown and slid his clasped hands down and under her belly. Roars of cheers and applause rose to meet their ears. It was truly a fun event for everyone.

The luncheon was very nice and the first time she'd spoken one on one with anyone about the baby. People wanted to know if she wanted a boy or girl, if she thought it was one or the other, what names they would use. Katrina laughed and said they hadn't gotten that far, but she and Markus would come to a decision soon and let them know. She took a few minutes with each young lady applying for the position of lady in waiting and narrowed it down to three. She introduced, in turn, each one to the queen for her inspection. After discussion, they decided that her new lady in waiting would be Lady Matilda of Southerby. She really connected with Katrina and seemed at ease while being very respectful. She had younger siblings so she should be very good with children as well.

That night Katrina and Markus decided they needed to discuss those things. He was told of her selection and advised Lady Matilda would be arriving in a week. She would share the room with Lady Alicia and a room was being readied for Lady Penelope, as she was the senior and her hours were much different than the other girls. "Have you thought about names for our baby?" Katrina began. "I know if it's a boy we would name it Nicholas Andrew Markus Jamison VI but what about a girl's name?" she asked "I kind of like Charlotte, what do you think of that?" he asked "I like it, what do you want to put with it?" she countered. "How about Annette?" Katrina exclaimed "I really like that Markus.

Charlotte Annette. It kind of has a nice ring to it. I think we've decided. We'll start spreading the word, everyone wants to know." she finished.

Markus was back to attending his regular duties and Katrina made occasional visits to see Lord Burtram and make sure the orphanage projects were on track. It seemed they were a well-oiled machine, the children loved the trade program. It gave them something to do for a few hours each day, as well as a promise of a self-sufficient future. So everyone was happy and the orphanage was making money too.

Alexander and Lady Penelope had fallen deeply in love with each other and were miserable that they could not start a life together. He couldn't do that to her and she didn't care. She loved him and if she had to see him in a prison cell the rest of her life, so be it. He was not as easily persuaded. They talked what ifs but they both didn't really think it would ever happen. They talked about the wedding, children, their beautiful home full of love. They knew deep down they were kidding themselves. If they wed, she would be allowed to visit and even conjugal visits would be allowed, but what kind of life could that be. Mommy bringing the children to see their father in prison. The children being ridiculed and ashamed of him. He just couldn't do it.

He tried to get her to stop coming, but she loved him too much. We'll just continue like we are she'd tell him. That was more than he'd ever hoped for since his first day in that cell. Maybe after the queen was gone and more people had died off that would remember, they could quietly pardon him and set him free, but that would be a long wait, probably too long to think about having children.

Katrina came to visit him weekly and usually brought Anne Marie. It was almost like a party when they came, so much sumptuous food, laughter and great stories. He'd painted a new picture of Anne Marie and Katrina, and made her promise to bring the baby as soon as possible so he could do a new family portrait. The queen wanted a new portrait done as well, he'd been deciding what to do about that for quite a while now. He didn't mind doing it, but was sure she wouldn't want to come to the prison. This whole situation seemed impossible. It's like he was free, but yet contained in this one room. He felt like a prisoner, but then again he had so much more luxuries and advantages than a regular prisoner, he felt like a free man. If he could only get his heart on board with his head!

Chapter 16 - The Truth

Fall came and went, winter was mostly over and spring was just around the corner. Katrina was huge; all in the belly, but huge none-the-less. She had gained so much weight with this child it didn't seem possible. She was constantly being kicked and punched by its little legs and arms. It seemed to not have enough room to move around. The baby seemed to get so excited when Markus would touch her stomach and talk to it. It would kick double time, like it was dancing or something. Her time had come, so any day now, or any hour, she could go into labor and bring a beautiful new baby into the world. She had taken to wobbling when she walked and always had someone at her side, just in case she lost her balance. "I think this baby is going to be as big as Anne Marie when it comes out." She told Markus one afternoon. "I'm just so tired all the time. Aunt Lilly said that was a good sign we're almost ready" Markus tried to comfort her as best he could. He could guess, but really had no idea how she felt or just how much pain and discomfort she was in. She was so beautiful though, maybe more so when she carried his children.

It was the very morning after that conversation that her pain started. Anne called for Nanny Gertrude, the doctor, and Aunt Lilly to get ready. They had rags prepared, water boiling, wooden spoons for her to bite down on while pushing the baby. Hard labor sometimes caused broken teeth in women. They just didn't realize how hard they were biting down, it just helped with the pain. Aunt Lilly stayed by her head, rubbing her shoulders and back while giving her ginger tea between each episode. The doctor said everything was fine and he'd be back tomorrow, or send for him if he was needed; but he was sure Nanny Gertrude and the ladies could handle everything from here. It shouldn't be too long now. He was right, in a matter of four hours, Katrina delivered the most beautiful baby boy she'd ever laid eyes on. While Anne and Nanny Gertrude were attending to the afterbirth, Katrina was holding her son.

All of a sudden a huge pain hit her and Nanny Gertrude started screaming like a mad woman. "It can't be! Oh God, why are you punishing me! She kept screaming something, but the words were inaudible, she screamed like she was in pain, like someone had cut her leg off, like she was scared to death, all simultaneously. They couldn't get her to stop screaming, so they pulled her out of the way and as Katrina was bearing down to expel the afterbirth, Anne moved into position just in time to catch the second baby boy coming out. Nanny Gertrude was still screaming, pulling her hair, praying for mercy, rocking back and forth and hiding her head under her shawl.

She seemed like an animal that had been shot with an arrow but could not die.

Anne cleaned the second boy and laid him beside the first in Katrina's arms. They both had dark hair and eyes just like their daddy. Even the same nose. They were perfect specimens of a male baby.

At the first sound from Nanny Gertrude, Markus had burst into the room and was at Katrina's side holding her hand when the second baby was born. He couldn't believe she'd had twins. No wonder she'd gotten so big, there were two babies in there! It was amazing. She was exhausted, but just as happy.

"I know I told you, you'd better have some boys next, but I didn't know you were going to have them together." Markus told her." He kissed her and took the first baby. Anne gave him a cord to tie around his foot until they could figure out a better way to tell them apart. He was the oldest and first heir to the throne. After a few minutes of cuddling, Aunt Lilly took the babies and truly washed them proper and put them together in the crib. As she left to do this, she told Katrina to rest as they'd both be hungry in a very short while.

True to her word, she brought them back within the hour to be fed, taking each back to his bed when he was properly fed, burped and changed. She then returned to help Katrina with a bath. Markus knew she was not strong enough to help, so he stripped her and lifted her into the warm tub. He washed, dried and dressed her. Carrying her back to the settee near the fire so Lady Alicia could dry and fix her hair. Katrina fell asleep before she was finished.

Nanny Gertrude would not be consoled. She was still screaming. She sounded like a banshee, constant screaming and wailing. Crying she was sorry, praying for God to forgive her, shoving anyone away who tried to talk to her. This went on for two more hours and Markus had had all he could take. He went in, picked her up and carried her to another room on the other side of the palace. He instructed Lady Matilda to sit far down the hall and alert him if she stopped carrying on. It was another three hours before she stopped; probably too hoarse to scream any longer. Matilda came and got him. He went in to see if she was still alive and what had happened to her. All she would choke out was things were terribly wrong and she needed to tell them about it. She asked him to get the queen, Alexander, himself and Katrina together so she would only have to tell it once. Markus tried to persuade her to tell him, but she would not, she'd just start crying and screaming again. Things like she was going to rot in Hell for what she'd done, and they'd string her up when they found out. Along with I'm sorry between every other sentence. The front of her dress was soaked from the tears and she was still shaking.

He left her and went to tell his mother of all that had transpired. They couldn't imagine what had snapped in her head, but it was big and if this is what it took, then she'd send for Alexander to come and they'd sit down with her to find out what was wrong.

It was less than an hour before they were all seated and Markus carried Nanny Gertrude into the room and sat her in a chair at the end of Katrina's bed with everyone else gathered at the sides of the bed. "Now old woman, what has happened? I know it can't be about the babies, they are both perfect and Katrina is fine, so what set you to acting like you'd lost your mind?" he asked rather annoyed at her display. She was nearly a hundred years old, she should not be acting this way.

She took a deep breath and began to speak "I want you to know how sorry I am and I had hoped to never reveal my secret, but God gave you those babies and showed me I had to confess and repent of my sins, or I would rot in Hell and I still may." She looked at each of them before speaking again. "Your Highness" she addressed the queen, "When you were having your Markus, your sister-in-law was in the other room having her baby. She was further along than you and had her baby first." "Yes, Alexander." The queen interrupted. "Don't get ahead of my story." Nanny Gertrude continued. "When her baby was born, it was dead and as it came, she died as well, with blood gushing from within. It couldn't be stopped, but I didn't have time to tell anyone about it because you were screaming in pain and your baby was coming. I rushed into your room and delivered Markus. He was a beautiful baby and as I was attending to the afterbirth, another baby was born. You were not paying attention to what I was doing and I was the only one who saw. Your brother had lost so much, his wife and child in the same minutes, I just couldn't let that happen to him. He needed something to hold on to life for; so I wrapped your second baby with the afterbirth and took him into the other room with me."

"I then went out to tell your brother his beloved had given her life producing his heir. I gave him your baby. He wept over his wife and accepted his son as the last thing his wife could do for him. He named him Alexander and raised him as his own. He never knew. Your Highness, Alexander is your second son. I've kept this hidden all these years and had I not feared for my immortal soul, it would still be my secret."

"Alexander, I am so sorry I lied about you and to you all these years. I stole your mother from you. I know you were happy and you loved your father very much, but that was not a decision I should have made. Can you ever forgive me? I beg your forgiveness. All of you. I've wronged you all. I've been conceited all these years and bragged about being the best mid-wife in the kingdom. I just couldn't face you all, so I did the only service I could for you—deliver babies and look after the mother." She buried her head in her lap and started crying again and they all looked at each other, stunned beyond belief.

After a few minutes of sobbing, she raised her head, took a deep breath and continued "I fully expect to be flogged, executed, or at least spend my final days in prison for what I've done. I gladly accept any punishment you have to offer me as I've been in misery for years, especially when this business all happened and Alexander was cast into prison. I should have done something then, but I just could not bring myself to say the words. To tell the horrible thing I had done." She dropped to her knees on the floor and cried out for forgiveness to them and to God. She screamed again how sorry she was for causing so much pain. She finally looked up at the queen and continued speaking between sobs. "It was the only thing I knew to do, you and she were so close, like sisters, this would be your gift to her. You would never know you'd given your son so no harm could happen from it all. I was wrong, I was so wrong." She finished in sobs again.

Markus moved to Alexander and hugged him. "We always were like brothers. No wonder we felt such a connection, we actually were!" "It's hard to believe." Alexander said as he hugged him in return. "It makes sense in a lot of ways, your mother, er our mother, always had a special bond with me and I with her. I just thought it was because I had no mother. It also makes sense because we are identical. It always seemed impossible that cousins could be totally identical. Had I not been told of her hysterics and seen her tell the story, I may still not have believed it, but now I do and I believe it's true." He turned toward the queen "Mother, will you accept me as your own? He asked. She was already crying and had started to rise. She met him halfway and they embraced. "Of course Alexander, you always were like my son anyway. No wonder I loved you so much, you were and are my flesh!" "I'd asked Markus to tell you I wanted to apologize to you for what I'd done, but with all the commotion, we never got together for me to do it. I truly am sorry Mother. I should have listened long ago when people tried to tell me the whole story." He finished with tears streaming down his face. "No need to worry over it now. All is well, my son." She said as she embraced him again.

Now there were tears streaming down everyone's face.

Alexander and the queen walked toward Nanny Gertrude and helped her stand. The queen looked her square in the eyes and said "While it is reprehensible this thing you have done, you did it with kindness in your heart at the time, so I decree you to be pardoned from your sins, but you are not to be allowed present at the birth of any child ever again. Instead of a prison cell, you will remain confined to your home for the rest of your days." "Thank you, thank you, thank you my queen, your mercy is everlasting. Long live the queen!" she exclaimed as tears of relief filled her eyes and fell down her cheeks again. Everyone responded "Long live the queen!"

The queen turned back to Alexander and began her next decree "Alexander" she again took his hand "I pardon you from all acts of treason and restore any property you have. I give you my estate in Hamsburg for your very own. You have been wronged your entire life, but only from a lack of knowledge of what was right. You will be a free man from this minute. I wish you to remain here until you so choose to visit or move to your estate. I now have my whole family with me. I love you son." She said through her tears, and hugged him again.

They rang for the butler to see Nanny Gertrude home and then proceeded to talk about this turn of events. They each took turns holding the babies. Katrina spoke up and interrupted all conversation. "We have a name for the eldest, he'll be the sixth, but we need a name for our second son. Alexander, would you be averse to us naming him after you and King Rupert, of course?" she asked smiling. "Actually I have plans for that name now that I'm a free man, if it pleases your highness to allow such a thing. I am a man in love and would like to start a family with my beautiful Lady Penelope if I can have approval from my mother, the queen." He glanced at her and she was already nodding her head with tears running down her face.

They called for Lady Penelope to be brought into the room. Alexander explained to her the turn of events. She began crying; knowing he would be free meant everything to her. When he'd finished explaining, he asked if she had any questions. When she shook her head no while wiping more tears away. Alexander got down on one knee in front of her and said "I have one question left. Will you marry me Lady Penelope and make me the happiest man on earth?" She leaped from her chair into his arms and squeezed him like her life depended on it. "Of course I will, Alexander! I love you with all my heart!"

Everyone cheered and Markus said, we'll need to contact her father and start making plans, but first, let's take care of all these tears and have some food. It's been hours since we've eaten, and I am famished. I know Katrina must be and most everyone else here has been at her side. We have some celebrating to do! We also have to choose a name for our son, if anyone has any ideas, we'll discuss them while we eat. Mother, that especially means you." He smiled and they all started toward the dining room. Markus picked Katrina up and carried her there. She was starving and had rested enough to sit at the table to eat. It was the biggest happiest group that had ever eaten at that table. Katrina had insisted that Aunt Lilly, Anne, Ladies Alicia and Penelope eat with them as well. Lady Matilda watched the children. Lilly and Anne were so honored by the request that they join the family for lunch, they felt truly appreciated and loved by them all.

Lunch was more like a family reunion than a "we just had a baby" party. With Alexander now back with them and he and Lady Penelope about to get married, there was so much buzz between everyone, it was hard to follow all the conversations.

Finally Markus declared "We're all going to make notes and lists of what we want and we'll meet for dinner and discuss all the things we need to do." Everyone agreed that was a splendid idea, so they all set off to their own rooms or sitting rooms to talk in couples about what needs and problems they had to resolve.

Markus carried Katrina back to her bed and ordered her to sleep for an hour. "I can't sleep now Markus!" she told him, we have lists to compile. Please get my lap desk, paper and quill. We have many things to be decided rather quickly and the first on our list is the name of our son." "You're right dear." He countered. When finished, their list consisted of the following:
1. Name for our son.
2. Move Alexander's things to the palace, his old room would be prepared.
3. Send word for Lady Penelope's parents to come for dinner.
4. Prepare birth announcement once the name was decided.
5. Select a wedding date and start preparations for that blessed event.
　　　Musicians
　　　Priest
　　　Food
　　　Dress
　　　Attendants
　　　Decorations

They were sure most of these would overlap Alexander and Penelope's list, but that was ok, they'd work it out together.

Everyone was so excited by dinnertime, they could hardly wait for the bell to sound dinner was ready. They'd calmed down some and weren't chattering among themselves, but were having their conversations in a more orderly manner.

Over dinner they decided upon a name for the baby. He was to be called Frederick Arthur Rupert Jamison. They definitely wanted to call him Frederick. There was a brief discussion of the name and what relative it honored. Penelope declared she was marrying Alexander but didn't even know his full name. When he told her it was Thomas Alexander Edmund Jamison, she said she loved it and Katrina caught her breath. "You didn't tell me Thomas was part of your name when I chose that for our baby. You just said it was a family name. I'm so glad that worked out because unknowingly I named our baby after the one who saved me when I'd have lost my mind over losing it.

As the next course was being served, Lady Penelope leaned over and asked Katrina, how she could tell them apart, they truly were identical. In the prison, in prison clothes, it had been easy to tell them apart, but with Alexander cleaned up and in proper attire, she really couldn't tell which was which. They looked and sounded exactly alike. One could easily pose for the other. Katrina explained

Markus had a scar and gave her the short version of the story. She told her that was the only true way that she could tell them apart if one were trying to be the other, like when Alexander was trying to take over the kingdom.

When Alexander decided his old room would be wonderful. Markus rang for the butler and advised him to ready it for Alexander and to have all his supplies moved here from the prison. "The adjoining room will be perfect for you to paint in, if you wish. It has a lot of natural light since it faces east, so let's have his studio there." Alexander chimed in with "Perfect! I was just thinking the same thing. Thank you brother!" at that, the queen spoke up "We can make the whole wing at your disposal son, if you'd like to stay here a while even after your wedding takes place. It's so good to have everyone together." "Penelope and I will discuss it mother, thank you for the invitation." "You are welcome to anything I have son, I hope you know that." She smiled and continued. "Now, when do you want to have Penelope's parents here for dinner and how big an affair would you like?"

"I'm thinking just family, mother, if that's alright. I don't know how much they know about me and we'll have to explain how we are actually twins. I think that would be easier if it's a smaller group, then once we have their blessings, we can have an engagement party." Alexander finished and looked at Penelope for her approval. "I think that's perfect!" she chimed in. The queen rang for her assistant and gave instructions for the birth announcement to be prepared for her to sign and for a dispatch to be sent to Penelope's family inviting them to dinner in four days." She looked at Alexander regarding the date and he nodded his approval.

"Now," the queen smiled, "let's get to deciding on wedding arrangements, that's always the fun part. Do you two have a date in mind now that you've had a few hours to talk things over?" "We do mother. If it's okay with Markus and Katrina, we'd like to be wed on April 20th. It's not far off and it seemed to be a good day for you two. Plus I did almost get married that day once before." He joked.

They all laughed. It was good to be able to joke about it now. It was such a horrible time for them all, but now would be a wonderful date for both couples to remember. "Splendid!" Markus exclaimed. May it bring you both the same joy it has brought to us. But you are aware, that's just about six weeks to pull it all together?" "We know, but we don't want to wait any longer and with everyone's help, I think we can do it." Alexander answered.

Katrina was the one who spoke this time as she

turned to the butler. "Have Anne dispatch a courier to my favorite dressmaker telling her she is needed here at the palace to make another wedding dress. We need her to bring two assistants and all the fabrics she has in stock for a trousseau. We'll need the wedding gown first, but will need many other dresses as well. There are the attendants, her mother, your mother, my dress, Anne Marie's dress and the trousseau. Tell her it is a personal favor for me." She then turned to Penelope. "I think that will take care of the gown, except for you and I designing it tomorrow. I also think you should get that young girl, Ariel, to sing at your wedding, she was amazing at the Wee Ball. I think our cook can take care of all the foods and cake needed. If you have something specific you want Penelope, just let her know. Alexander, you'll need to talk to the priest. Mother, I think if you and Penelope get together on decorations, maybe invite her mother and sisters to contribute, that can be knocked out pretty fast too." "Wow Katrina, You sure know how to pull a wedding together fast!" Markus exclaimed. "Well, when a girl's about to get what she's wanted for so long, it's time to jump into action and make things happen." She laughed and winked at Penelope. She blushed slightly and the rest of them laughed again. It was going to be a whirlwind, but that wouldn't matter, it was a joyous time and everyone wanted it to happen as quickly as Alexander and Penelope did.

It was late when they finally retired from dinner. Katrina had two fussy boys by the time she reached her room. They were both wanting fed. "Oh Markus, this is going to be a challenge. Two at one time and Anne Marie is just past two, she's still a baby too." I know you can handle it, my love, and you have the amazing Aunt Lilly to help you, along with Lady Matilda. It will be fine. I won't be able to feed them for you, but I can help with many other things, like baths. You know how much I like to bath you." He grinned. "Just about as much as I like you to." She responded. They kissed deeply as their sons had their dinner. "We've got a good life Markus, and now a brother and sister of our very own."

The next morning, after breakfast Katrina and Penelope began designing her dress. She held the babies for a while and exclaimed how she wished they'd have their own very soon. She was so happy. She asked Katrina some questions about her wifely duties and thanked her for her candor. Katrina told her she knew Alexander would be gentle with her because he loved her so much, and she knew their life would be wonderful together.

The dinner was uneventful, other than explaining how that Alexander was now a free man and now fourth in line for the throne. Penelope's parents felt much better about the situation and gave their blessing. Alexander was a real charmer and they liked him very much. Rooms were made available for them to stay a few days to contribute their ideas for the wedding and be fitted for gowns. The tailor was called to do suits for the men once Penelope decided what colors she wanted to use.

The only thing she asked the cook for was lemon cookies since they were Alexander's favorite dessert. The cook informed her that it was the lemon he loved, so they decided to make the wedding cake lemon and since it was springtime and keeping with that theme, the attendants dresses would be a soft buttercup yellow, and the bouquets would be calla-lilies and buttercups.

Chapter 17 – Another Beginning

It was finally April 20th and all was well in
the world. Everyone was anticipating the
wedding of the year. The reception was at the
palace, of course, following the ceremony which
was at the church.

Katrina and Lady Alicia were helping
Penelope dress. They pulled her hair up in
loose curls on her head, with tiny wisps and
tendrils hanging down to frame her face and
tease the back of her neck. She wore a
beautiful yellow gold tiara and the queen's
Canary diamond necklace. They matched the
theme perfectly. Her dress was everything a
princess' gown should be. Katrina's seamstress'
team had outdone themselves. They'd created
a wedding gown, three attendant gowns,
twelve dresses and undergarments for
Penelope's trousseau, a dress for Anne Marie,
one for the mother of the bride and one for the
queen all in a little over six weeks The tailor
had equally stepped up to the challenge.

Penelope and Katrina had designed her
wedding gown. It was off the shoulder and the
bodice was covered in lace with tiny pearls
sewn on the front looking like a waterfall,
patterned from the center of her breasts
flowing out to the waist. The skirt looked like
petals with layer after layer of small pieces
of sheer silk sewn all the way to the floor,

overlapping each other. They fluttered when she walked. It was sort of bell shaped and had a double train coming from her waist and then again from her shoulders. The veil on her head was long in the back and the edging was the same tiny petals along the edge. She wore it covering her face to symbolize her purity and hinting at her groom's anticipation of whether it were his true love or not hidden behind that veil. He would lift it as the ceremony started.

It was a beautiful day for it and everyone was so happy. Crowds lined the street trying to catch a glimpse of the happy couple. Cheers erupted as the first coach appeared carrying the two princes and Alexander's other two attendants, his soon to be brothers-in-law. They waved to the crowds and entered the church, taking their appropriate places.

The next coach held the queen, Princess Anne Marie, Princes Nicholas and Frederick, Anne and Aunt Lilly. The queen stopped to accept some bouquets of flowers from some children in line to see them. She had the ladies hold the babies up for those fortunate enough to catch a glimpse as she herself held Anne Marie's hand and walked with her down the aisle to their seats.

Excitement was building as each coach approached in turn. The next held Penelope's parents, who were thoroughly enjoying the attention. Her father escorted her mother in, then returned to the entrance to escort Penelope in for the ceremony when she arrived.

Katrina, Lady Alicia, and Penelope's sister was in the next coach and when they began to exit, the crowd went crazy, they loved Katrina from the first time they saw her and certainly were not shy in letting her know it. People had flowers for her, baby things to give her and just wanted to receive a handshake or a wave from her. She had to have the driver collect the things and put them in the coach for her. She received so many compliments and well wishes as well as congratulations on the boys. She reminded them it was Lady Penelope's day and she would be following very shortly and she hoped they were as kind and generous to her as well. After all, she too was marrying a prince.

Alexander had opted for a black suit with a buttercup colored shirt and black tie. He was stunning as he stood there waiting for his bride.

Ariel had sung as Penelope and her attendants came down the aisle, again an amazing per-formance. First, was Penelope's sister, then Lady Alicia, Katrina and finally Penelope. Markus stood by Alexander's side along with Penelope's two brothers, all in the same attire as Alexander. The Queen had been royally seated on the front row with Aunt Lilly and Anne holding Anne Marie, and the babies, Nicholas and Frederick. Penelope's parents were seated on her side of the church, along with her grandmother and younger sister.

 The priest had gone through much of the ceremony, and was just to the final parts "Prince Thomas Alexander Edmund Jamison, do you take Lady Penelope of Manchester to be your wedded wife?" he asked

"I do." He said with a huge smile on his face.

"Do you Lady Penelope of Manchester, take Prince Thomas Alexander Edmund Jamison to be your husband" she hesitated. She turned to face Alexander, reached over and unbuttoned one button on his jacket and slipped her hand inside. She felt for the scar and when she found none, she quickly answered "I DO! For now and forever." She looked back at Alexander and said "With all that's happened in our lives, good and bad. I knew it was you, but I had to be sure."

Thank you so much for reading my novel. If you haven't read "Scars of the Heart" it precedes this one, but both are stand-alone books. I hope you enjoyed the read and love my characters as much as I do. If you wouldn't mind, would you kindly leave a review on any or all of the below sites:

Amazon.com
Goodreads.com
Author Kathy Roberts on Facebook

It helps others know if it's something they'd like to read, plus your feedback will help me improve with every story I write.

I love hearing your thoughts and comments as well. You are the reason we writers write!

Kathy